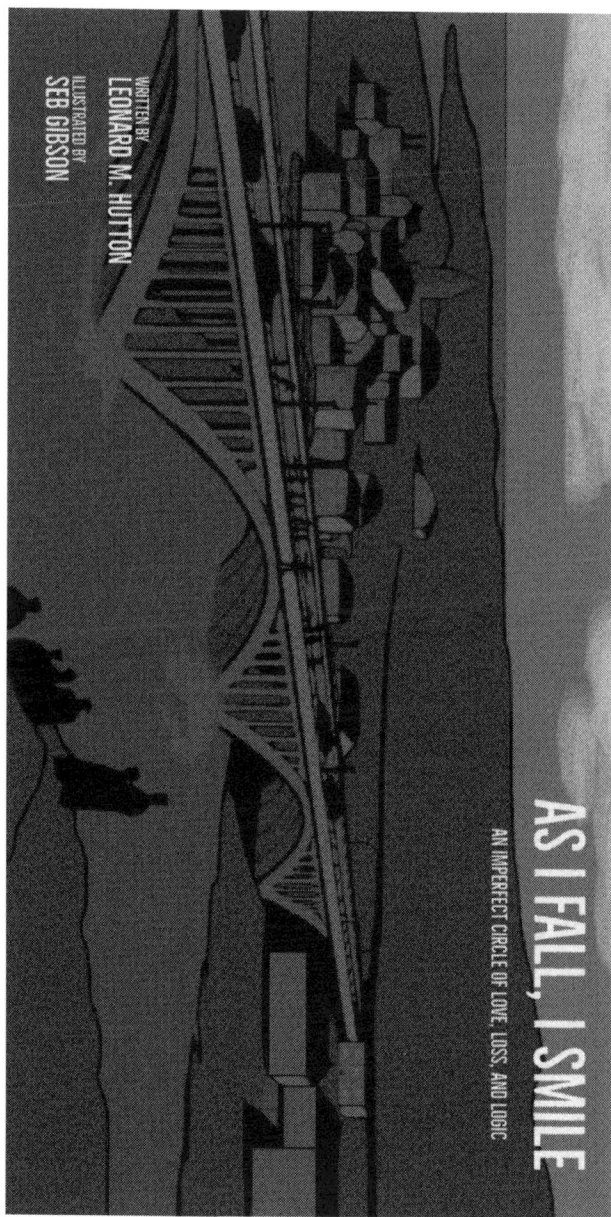

AS I FALL, I SMILE

AN IMPERFECT CIRCLE OF LOVE, LOSS, AND LOGIC

WRITTEN BY
LEONARD M. HUTTON

ILLUSTRATED BY
SEB GIBSON

Disclaimer

_This is a work of fiction. Names, characters,
businesses, events and incidents are the
products of the author's imagination. Any
resemblance to actual persons, living or dead,
or to actual events is purely coincidental. This
novel's story and characters are fictitious.
Certain long-standing institutions, agencies,
and public offices are mentioned, but the
characters involved are wholly imaginary. The
opinions expressed are those of the characters
and should not be confused with the author's,
even if some of them happen to be
synchronised._

Copyright

About the Author

Leonard M. Hutton is originally from Middlesbrough, North Yorkshire. He moved to North Northumberland at the age of three with his parents and older brother. He was educated locally, completing his A-Levels before going on to study Chinese Language at university.

After university he took on many jobs, from a jeweller to working as a mechanic. Though his main passion has always been for writing, poetry and literature, it wasn't until the COVID-19 crisis that he finally had the opportunity to properly codify many of his scattered chapters into a coherent body for publication.

He currently resides at his home in Lincolnshire with his wife and two daughters.

For Kav.

RIP brother.

"It is an extravagant demand that a man who no longer cares to live for himself, should still go on living as a mere machine for the benefit of others."

ARTHUR SCHOPENHAUER

"The Edge... There is no honest way to explain it because the only people who really know where it is are the ones who have gone over."

HUNTER S. THOMPSON

As I Fall, I Smile

{Chapter 0}

|Spectacle|

In the end, on the bridge. I glare down at the endless river beneath me. It looks cold, as a good Scottish river should; cold and harsh. The soles from my worn-out military issue shoes have little grip here at the edge. They have long since lost the shine and sparkle of that episode. With a turning glance I regard the people standing behind the hastily deployed makeshift barriers. They watch me. Watch me fixed in place like a statue on the precipice. I feel like a spectacle at a zoo. In this case I have made the spectacle of myself. I am not hesitating. I am just waiting. Waiting for my body to catch up to what my mind has decided to do.

Some good Samaritan called the police after only a few minutes of me being up here. A few minutes more had brought the police and an accompanying crowd. One of the police officers tried to talk me down. The thought of being talked down from here is amusing. I didn't climb up here to just climb down again. And here I am. I see my wife, parted from the crowd, being consoled by a female police officer. She is teary, borderline hysterical. I also see some teens with smartphones poised. Cameras trained on me like social media snipers. No doubt they are hoping to get a viral sensation out of my descent.

I return my gaze to the water. I love the water. I always have. My earliest memories are of being in water. Being in a swimming pool with my father as he taught me how to swim. I remember him stepping backwards in the outdoor pool as I furiously kicked forward, amongst the sound of overfed seagulls, in an effort to catch him. I never did. It made me a strong swimmer. Living on an island an affinity for water was probably a good thing. All my life I have felt drawn to the water. Drawn to streams, rivers, to the sea. I think that's why of all the ways I have considered leaving this place, this is the way I have chosen. In one short sharp shock it will be over and done with: nothing but a splash and a body left behind. I'm sure that the emergency services will fish me out shortly afterwards. Perhaps they will even try to revive me. It will be a futile effort. The impact from this height will leave my body smashed and broken. Any body would be smashed and broken after this fall. The forces will be the same as if I landed on concrete. In all honesty, I'd prefer they just leave me in the river to float on out to the sea. Let me disappear and be carried by the strong currents into the depths of the North Sea. Though I don't suppose it really matters. By that time my shell will have no importance. My chance, my only chance. My only hope.

I feel the sharp blustery wind curl around my frame. I wobble. I hear the crowd stir. Gasps, random pleas of "Don't do it" and "Stop messing about fella."

It is time.

The shattered mechanism of my mind revolves around the chain of events that has led me here. I have walked this road in my head already, guided by my thesis. Now for the final physical act of my life. I suppose there is no harm in running through it again from the start. One last time.

{Chapter 1}

|Open Day|

My conditional offer was 180 UCAS points to get in to Llantarn University. Having visited the campus already, I knew it was definitely the place for me. I had intended to travel down, stay the night, attend the university Open Day, stay one more night then go home – a short scouting mission only. After a total of six days down there I finally returned home. Those six days had been fascinating and free. Meeting students en masse in their natural habitat was a real eye-opener. Conversations I could scarcely imagine flowed commonplace from those junior intellectual mouths. The campus itself, well, Wow! What a place. So old and intrinsically bound to the nature it was situated in. It was almost as though it had grown there, as opposed to it having being constructed by the hands of men.

After having been on the move for many hours to even get to Llantarn I wanted to just sit, be still for a moment and smoke. I was primarily a student of English literature at the time and had brought along my copy of the 1805 version of Wordsworth's 'Prelude'. Perched upon a bench in full view of the old buildings and grounds I opened it and began to read.

> *'OH, there is blessing in this gentle breeze,*
> *That blows from the green fields and from*
> *the clouds*
> *And from the sky; it beats against my cheek,*
> *And seems half conscious of the joy it gives.'*

His words sank into me as if he were right there reading them directly to me. I had read these words many times before, but now I was really digesting them for the first time. The sun was bright, the air was warm and it caressed my face with what could have been interpreted as divinity.

The university was kind enough to let me stay in one of the spare rooms they had in an accommodation hall for next to nothing. Not fully understanding the dynamics of university life I had asked a rather juvenile question whilst picking up my room key from the Porters' Lodge.

"Is there a time that I need to be in my room by at night?"

My question clearly amused the porters as they just sniggered and sneered,

"No boyo, you just do whatever you like. You can make up your own bedtime now."

Upon entering my allocated lodgings, which resembled a small Travelodge room, I dropped my overnight bag on the desk. As the room door slid stealthy shut behind me, I decided to fully take stock of my situation. Quickly and lustfully it dawned on me, I was eighteen years old, in an unfamiliar setting with my own room. I was in possession of a wallet with a few quid in it and nothing to do until ten o'clock the next morning. Naturally the first thing I wanted to do was explore. I had really done my research on the place. I'd had a copy of the university prospectus on my bedside table at home ever since I liberated it from the sixth form common-room at Woodbourne. I had committed many of the photographs from the website and prospectus to memory. There was a 360-degree camera view from the main tower of the Old Hall Building that you could access at any time through their webpage. Often during boring free periods at school, when I was supposed to be studying, I would log on and have another look. It seemed almost surreal to me to be finally walking around the paths I had seen so often on screen. Like that feeling you get when you see your hometown or street on the television.

I left my room and walked. I walked far slower than I normally would; walked amongst bizarre-looking people to my sheltered young eyes. Students just being students, busying themselves about their normal day. The buildings that straddled the walkways themselves seemed innately full of knowledge and memory. After an hour or so of bimbling around the campus lanes I came across the entrance to the Students' Union bar; it was at this time I made the informed and educated decision to get as smashed as possible.

My alarm sounded at nine o'clock. I sprang out of bed as only a spry teenager could, my youth keeping any form of hangover suppressed. Fresh-faced and keen-eyed I arrived at the Theology and Philosophy department with notebook and pencil in hand. I sat there for a few hours receiving briefs from department heads, current lecturers and students about to graduate. All the presenters reinforced my opinion that this place was for me. They all promoted the values of academic and social enrichment that bound me further to my choice. In truth, Llantarn was not a difficult university to get in to. It was not a university that was particularly well known nor seen as elite. It was perfectly happy being tucked away, isolated, in its little valley in deepest Wales, thirty miles away from the next conurbation of note.

The recollection of the previous evening's activities surfaced and reminded me that the students of Llantarn referred to life there as being in 'The Bubble'. 'The Bubble' was an abstract notion of reality in which events that happened in the outside world had little to no impact on life inside. Only things that occurred inside 'The Bubble' had affect or effect. Despite the twenty-first century being well underway, there was pitifully little television or radio reception down in the valley; word of mouth was the surest way to gain information. And people only really talked about what happened in Llantarn. With my desire to study philosophy I didn't think an up-to-date knowledge of world/current affairs would be altogether essential. Isolation from the wider world would suit me just fine.

I had spent a great deal of time debating with myself as to what I actually wanted to do with my life. I had stumbled onto the Llantarn prospectus whilst flicking through the ones for all the normal choices: Manchester, Durham, Newcastle, Edinburgh etc. But Llantarn was one I did not glance through. It was the one I actually read. I saw it and felt such an instantly strong attraction. As a result, I had been worried that my visit would be an underwhelming experience. To my unfounded joy that had not been the case. I was keener than ever. I departed Llantarn six days and scores of conversations later having woken up on a couple of random student sofas along the way. As I left, I knew exactly what I wanted to do and where I wanted to do it. I wanted to go to Llantarn; I wanted to study philosophy. I was so enamoured that I used all of my UCAS course bids to study there. The scholastic requirements were not too demanding for entry onto any of the courses I had applied for. Knowing that allowed me to really enjoy the last few months of my school time at Woodbourne. The last few months of my dwindling school career.

{Chapter 2}

|Woodbourne|

I had not been popular at school. I hadn't been unpopular either. Essentially, I wouldn't get invited to parties but if I turned up at them anyway, I wouldn't be asked to leave. The school itself was a grand old construction, full of stretching history that I had never bothered to investigate properly. I had started there at the age of twelve. Like most twelve-year-old boys I acted as though I were in my late teens. I was cynical beyond my years and always thought I knew best. I was unmotivated and uncommitted in any serious way to my studies - the only exception to that being certain parts of the English curriculum that I actually enjoyed. My lack of academic dedication was an extreme annoyance to my parents. A continuous litany of sub-mediocre grades had been all I could produce from my six hideously expensive years at Woodbourne, alongside the occasional disciplinary letter that rattled through the front door. My father was in a persistent bi-emotional state towards me, anger and disappointment.

"I pay bloody thousands for you to go to that school and all you seem to do is piss-fart about instead of applying yourself."

I would hear these words, or words in a similar vein regularly whilst at home. Being a self-made man it severely galled him to see me throwing away all of the opportunities that he had never been afforded but strived to provide for me. Certainly, looking back on it, he had a perfectly valid point.

Mother and Father had seemed more than slightly relieved when I came home one day clutching a prospectus and told them about wanting to go to Llantarn and study philosophy. *"Finally, some direction"* I could hear them think. University, graduation, academic achievement;

something my parents could shout about at the rowing club's annual dinner or church coffee morning. With that said, they were not too keen on the location of where I wanted to go. Not because it meant that I'd be on the other side of the country. But because the projected conversations would play out less satisfactorily than they had hoped:

"Oh yes, Peter is studying at University now."

"Oh, jolly good, whereabouts is he?"

"Peter is studying down in Llantarn."

"Where?"

"Llantarn, it's in South Wales."

"Oh, I see. Never heard of it."

Whereas the conversation they wanted to have was slightly different:

"Oh yes, Peter is studying at University now."

"Oh, jolly good, where abouts is he?"

"Peter is studying down in Durham/York/insert well known prestigious University."

"Oh, well, yes that's very impressive."

"Yes, we are all so very proud of him."

Alas, for them the latter was not going to be the case. My parents coped with the reality that I wouldn't be aiming my sights in the same direction as theirs and held onto the fact that at least I now had an aim of some kind. Ultimately, they were happy with me for once. I wasn't going to fall out of school and land straight at the job centre. I never had any intention of doing that, but there was no need to let them know that.

It was the spring of 2005. A-Level results day came around like a flash, almost as if the time since my Open Day visit hadn't even happened. Standing in line awaiting my brown envelope, I was observing some of my peers. The results were to be handed out in the main school entrance hall and this had produced quite a long queue trailing out from the main door into the green vista-blessed car park. Some of my fellow pupils that waited around me hoped and expected to get the straight A's required to be doctors, vets, etc. Some were trying to get into one of the 'Big Two'. I could only imagine the pressures - both parental and self-induced - that they must have experienced over the last four years that were now coming to a head. There were nervous faces everywhere to various degrees. In truth, even I was a tad apprehensive. It would still be a few minutes before the envelopes were due to be released. The grades I needed were not high, and I was reasonably sure I'd worked just about hard enough to get them. Still, I couldn't be sure. I also had no contingency plan, so if I didn't get into Llantarn I was pretty snookered. I would feel better once I had the grades in my hand, in black and white. Standing close to the entrance porch I cast my eyes around again, this time to look once more at the stunning grounds and stately manner of the school. I would come to miss it. It struck me how similar it was to Llantarn: isolated, rural, green in every direction. I suggested to myself that Llantarn was just the natural progression from Woodbourne.

"Alright Pete?" came a voice to my rear. A 'friend' named Darren, or more commonly just 'Daz' had cut in the place behind me. I'd been so lost in thought that I hadn't even noticed.

"Yeah not bad mate. You?" I responded. Daz and I had a friendship of convenience. We were both smokers. As a result of that fact we would commonly pool nicotine-related resources. We were always civil with one another and had been taking short trips to the walled garden orchards together for a couple of years. I could tell by the way he was gesturing at me that he wouldn't mind going for one before getting the results. He replaced his gesturing head with spoken confirmation.

"Might as well pop for a quick one now eh. For old times' sake?"

I interpreted his want for a nostalgic smoking stroll to mean that he didn't have any cigarettes of his own and was in need of supply. Having a mostly full pack in my pocket and always willing to pop for a smoke I replied.

"Aye could do I suppose. What's printed up on those papers isn't going to change now, is it? Besides, they haven't started handing them out yet. Probably just be hanging around for the same time we could be there and back again."

"Yeah, fair one," Daz said in passing as we departed for our short walk to blacken our young lungs.

I've always loved smoking. There's just something so reassuring and irreversible about watching the blue-grey smoke vector away in spiralling fractals. The view we had in our regular smoking haunt was beautifully peaceful. Never-ending green countryside, punctuated by an old B-road meandering its way through the fields like a stone river. Daz felt the need to butt in to my last chance to appreciate the view.

"Where did you say you were going again?" he asked referring to my university of choice. A conversation we had had at least five times previously.

"Llantarn," I said with a slight tone of desire in the thought of the place. I knew his next question would be, *"Where is that again?"*

"Where is that again?" he dutifully asked.

"South Wales," I replied, my tone neutral.

"Oh yeah, that's right. I remember you saying. You confident about getting what you need then?" he asked as he tapped away some ash to the ground.

"Yup." My tone was more staccato in the hope that it would have killed off the chat. It did not.

"Well, I'm hoping to get Lincoln."

"Yes, I know. To do media and hospitality studies." In another effort to halt the pointless chit-chat I tried to instigate the end of it by saying, "Well, good luck."

"Thanks, you too." And that was that. The last chat in the smokers' lair. The last wisps of Woodbourne. We finished our cigarettes in silence and I felt, after he had stopped talking, that he actually absorbed the sight too. With our butts stubbed out we made our way back to the main entrance.

Through the glass of the main door we saw people dancing around holding pieces of paper. One or two were sat shaking, close to tears or there already. Opening the large heavy wooden door of the main entrance a rush of sound hit us. Screams of delight dwarfed the sighs of disappointment.

Daz and I got handed our results together and so opened them simultaneously. Daz said nothing. His disappointment evident. Twisted facial grimaces accompanied a long exhalation from his nose. He would have to do some quick manoeuvring to find a course somewhere for him to study something. It later transpired that he was able to spell out the word, 'DUDE' with the grade awards he had been given. Oh well. He disappeared with Mr. Russett, the sixth form advisor, to make some rapid/desperate phone calls. I would never see him again.

Next, I felt a tap on my shoulder. It was Henrietta.

"4 A's Pete. I got 4 A's. I'm off to Durham." Henny was probably my best friend at Woodbourne. The feeling was not reciprocated. I'm sure that she did actually like me, unlike most of my peers, but Henny was extremely popular. She was undeniably beautiful, intelligent and characterful. We had grown slightly closer over the last couple years, but nowhere near as close as I would have liked. Yet, close enough so that she would actually refer to me as a friend.

"Congratulations," I managed to get out.

"How did you get on?" she asked with her gorgeous smile. I looked right into her eyes and answered.

"I am off to Llantarn."

{Chapter 3}

|Packing|

Mother and Father were reasonably happy. Though my results easily put me north of the required points I needed, they were still not worth bragging about. They thought I had set the bar so easily within reach that actually reaching it wasn't much of an achievement. I am sure they were sort of proud, in a way, but more so relieved. I have no idea how disappointed they'd have been if I had failed to reach that low bar. In any event, I did get what I needed. I was one summer away from university.

The summer of 2005 came and went, then the final evening at home arrived. I was in my room with empty boxes and full cupboards. Mother had instructed me to make three piles: the first I would take with me; the second would be winging its way to one of the local charity shops; the last would be kept in storage at home. I was never one for being particularly sentimental about material possessions. I was swift and ruthless in my pile construction. A lot of 'stuff' was heading to the charity shop. I even made a fourth pile of items to just chuck in the bin. I found it hard to think of things I'd actually need to take with me besides the obvious. I was going to study philosophy, so other than some books, some clothes, some bedding, a selection of notebooks and pencils, what else would I need? I also took my seldomly played guitar as it was a present from my parents and I was sure I'd get some free time to have a little strum now and then. I had one suitcase, one rucksack and one guitar. That was pretty much it. I went outside and loaded up my car. It didn't take long. I was sure it probably looked bare compared to most of the cars packed up by the other excited pre-students before they left for university.

I was happy that I had what I needed. It would be a bloody long drive down there. Rural Scotland to rural Wales. It would be the first time I had driven to Llantarn as for the Open Day I had elected to take public transport. It took a mere thirteen hours to get from door to door. Not an experience I wanted to repeat. Dwelling on the long nature of the drive to come I thought I had better 'borrow' some CDs from my father's study to keep me entertained along the way. I went inside his sanctum and stood in front of my father's impressive CD collection. I ran my fingers down the plastic spines of the cases as I read their titles, occasionally I pulled a disc or two free from the rack. Pink Floyd, Dire Straits, Peter Frampton, Led Zeppelin and a few others. They would complement my Oasis, Verve and Muse types rather nicely. I was going to have some loud variety on the long way south.

After claiming my audio bounty, I went into the living room and sat down on the sofa. Mother had just made a fresh pot of tea. A platter of homemade cherry scones with a spread of rich salted butter nestled on a gold trimmed plate atop a bright white doily. I knew that in the future I would occasionally miss these times. The freedom from bills, cooking, and the responsibility of having to administrate my own life. Such administration was a price I willingly paid to get to Llantarn and be a student. I felt butterflies rise inside my stomach at the knowledge of that being only a day away. Yet for all the excitement of the pressing adventure, I would miss home. I was never one for feeling severely homesick, I just wasn't the sort. But actually leaving home was a different circumstance, and I did love my parents, even if I had never really done much to show it. Yes, I would miss home.

Father walked into the room and strolled purposefully over to the old mahogany drinks cabinet pressed against the far wall. He opened it and extended the internal serving tray with one hand, the other reached for a bottle of Edradour. As he poured a generous serving into a crystal tumbler. He asked my mother, "Would you like anything my dear? A little drop of something?"

"Oh, go on then," she replied. Unusually in the affirmative as I had rarely seen my mother imbibe alcohol. "Pour me a small dry sherry." Father did not offer me anything. I had an early start and a long drive. In his mind a single drink the night before was an unwarranted risk. I didn't mind.

I had an upcoming Freshers' Week where having a non-alcoholic drink would no doubt prove to be challenging. Father sat down in his cherry Chesterfield chair. He raised his glass toward me and my mother replicated his action.

"Well, good luck Peter," expressed Father as he charged his glass. Mother took a small sip then spoke.

"Yes, good luck son. Make sure that you work hard and don't waste the money you have on drink and cigarettes." Her repetitive lecture began again. The kind of lecture that made me want a drink and a cigarette. "Make sure that you have at least one proper meal a day. Not something that comes out of a microwave. Cook for yourself and don't be eating in cafés or having lots of takeaways." I settled down with my 'receiving a lecture face' on. "Don't go stupid on the drink because you'll end up in hospital and you'll get yourself a criminal record and bring shame on us all."

My mother was one of life's natural born worriers. Often during the school holidays I would just get up, pull on my hiking boots and disappear for the day into the countryside. I wouldn't take my phone with me and she'd be in an irrational tizz upon my return. Her mind used to play such negative games on her when I wasn't contactable or in sight. She would just say "I'm a mother. It's what we do," which I am sure was true to some degree, but not to the extent she took it to. The way she gave me the current lecture made me feel like the sentence, "and don't talk to strangers" was on the tip of her tongue. It would be a while before I'd have to endure one of her lectures again in person. Thank the Lord!

As I lay in my bed that night, I was excited. I pulsated at the prospect of the next day. My mind rolled over all the things I was eager to see and do. Things like reading by the river that flowed through the campus, the Freshers' Week parties, all the people I was going to meet. Innumerable perspectives and opinions all waiting to be heard. When I did sleep, it was the light sleep of an excited young man.

{Chapter 4}

|Croeso|

My eyes flashed open with the first electro-howl of my alarm. The time, 06:00, was beaming into my room in blood-red digital light. I was never one for early mornings. At six o'clock in the AM my body told me that the natural place for it be was right where it already was, in bed. Perhaps I'd had some mattress DNA implanted into me during my conception. My body was begging me to turn over and return to sleep, my mind took a minute or so to spool up. As it did the rampant butterflies kicked in. There was no rolling over today. My brain took firm control of the urges in my body and lifted me out of bed. The curtains were opened, the lamp was flicked on, my eyes strained for a moment. I reasoned that a shower was the ideal mode to completely switch me on and get me ready for whatever the day had in store. I walked across my room and plucked a towel from its hanger and headed to the upstairs bathroom. The clock read 06:02.

As I stepped out of the shower the bathroom clock read 06:33. I always felt better after a good shower. It's just nice to feel clean, fresh and ready. I exited the bathroom and headed along the corridor back to my room. Paraded either side of me on the walls and tables were the assembled ranks of family photographs set in ornate frames. Three years' time and there would be one of me alongside them, holding my degree, mortarboard and all. There would be a lot of work to do before then. Lots of reading and writing. At the time I thought it was best to just focus on physically getting to the university before picturing where my graduation photograph would feature on the family wall.

I opened my bedroom door and dried myself as thoroughly and hastily as possible. I caught a glance of myself in the mirror and allowed myself a moment of personal introspection. I just stood there and stared myself in the eyes. In the growing clarity of the morning light I said out loud to myself, "Today's the day." I gave myself a shake and went to brush my teeth. With teeth brushed I reached for the clothes I had prearranged on the chair in my room the previous night. I had prepared my trusty faded black jeans, white boxers, plain black woollen socks, a fairly tightly fitted white t-shirt, and an old-fashioned black blazer. I was going for the smart casual modern student look. My jeans were a little too loose and my t-shirt a little too tight so that it revealed my bony, rather than muscular physique. I applied a swift blast of wet-look hair gel and felt ready to go. I thought I looked pretty cool at the time; in retrospect, I probably looked like a pretentious skinny twat. As I switched off the bedroom light, I saw the glowing time again: 07:08.

I had planned to leave no later than eight o'clock. The online route map my father had printed out for me stated it would take approximately eight hours to drive from start to finish. My father was well aware of the fact that I had a satnav in the car which hadn't let me down so far, but he was very much a 'belt and braces' man. I planned to rest a couple of times for half an hour or so along the way, but I would see how I felt once I got on the road. I entered the kitchen and saw Mother and Father sat at the breakfast table wearing their usual morning regalia of pyjamas, dressing gowns and slippers.

"Morning son," led Mother with a cheery disposition.

"Morning," I replied. Father remained silent with his head buried in the newspaper, slowly sipping his cup of tea. I sat adjacent to him at the table and he looked at me as he carefully placed his paper down onto the table.

"Did you sleep well then?" he asked - whether out of civility or genuine query I didn't know.

"Yes thank you." I responded with the same level of cheer as had been exhibited by my mother. "I doubt that the bed I will get in my uni room will be anywhere near as comfortable though." With that statement I had invited my father to open up a line of conversation with me about my accommodation or whether I had packed any bedding; anything. He responded with,

"Mmmm, no. Probably not." My father had always been a man of few words, or at least ever since I had known him. I was sure that he did care about me, but the occasional pat on the shoulder was all that he'd deign to use to show that care. I guess he was just what many would describe as a 'proper' man. He didn't really do feelings, just practicalities. Whilst my father didn't talk a lot about emotions, he was always happy to point out what he thought I was doing wrong.

"If I were you, I'd have been up at five and been halfway down the road by now. You'll catch bad traffic going past Carlisle by leaving at eight." Unlike me, my father was always an early riser. I gave no retort to his observation regarding my apparently tardy departure time. I had often thought that I was a disappointment to him. In addition to that, I had thought that he must have been disappointed in himself for not being able to raise an ultra-competitive and proactive son with a devout work ethic and strong jawline. I was sure a significant part of him regretted me. But he was still my father and I his son. Before I could dwell any further down those lines of thought Mother had placed a large plate in front of me. Bacon, sausage, black pudding, haggis, potato scones, fried bread, and two fried eggs. Along with the fry-up came a pint glass nearly full to the brim of fresh orange juice.

"There you go love. That should set you up nicely for the day." She said it with the same cheerfulness that had greeted me when I entered the kitchen. I was hungry. Fortunately I had the appetite of a growing teenager and possessed one of those metabolisms that, so far, meant I could eat and eat without putting on any weight. I voiced my appreciation.

"Thanks very much. I'm going to miss you being around to make me breakfast."

"Oh yes, I bet you are. You'll miss me cooking for you, and washing up, cleaning and ironing for you all the time." She hadn't declared it with any malice, only with light humour. My mother was a career house wife. She had genuinely loved keeping the house ship-shape and running smoothly. My father did not pick up on the light humoured nature of my mother's last comment. He simply looked over at me and delivered a 'hmm' sound, as if he was just agreeing with my mother in a factual way. I tucked into my delightful breakfast feast and relished every bite. By the time I was able to polish off the last morsel I caught sight of the kitchen clock on the wall. 07:36. I stood up.

"Best be getting on my way now," I asserted before downing the last of my orange juice.

Mother shared a look with my father and spoke.

"Well, wait just a minute. Your father and I have got a little something for you."

"For your studies," Father injected sternly.

"Oh yes?" I questioned inquisitively. I expected a dictionary or some other academically associated gift. Such gifts had been common for me down the years and had formed the mainstay of birthdays and Christmases, apart from the car they had given to me when I had turned seventeen of course.

"Here you go," announced Father as he produced a brand-new laptop computer. Expressions of surprise and genuine gratitude were written all across my face.

"Wow, that's very, wow! Thank you. Thank you both so much. This day just keeps getting better." I restrained my obvious elation at the new toy as best as I could. I was conscious that I needed to justify my father's financial expenditure, so I stated quite properly, "This will be invaluable for completing my course."

"Well," Father began, "I just hope that you take full advantage of this piece of equipment and take the time to look after and maintain it properly. It comes with a comprehensive operating manual. I am told it is a good quality machine and trust that it will serve your requirements in full. It also comes with this case for you to be able to transport it safely." Father's eyes narrowed.

"Ensure you use it. I don't want to see you with it at Christmas and for it to have a large crack running down the screen." The time read 07:45.

Before leaving I decided to have a look around the house. As stated, I had never suffered from being terribly homesick and I'd be back here in just over three months for Christmas, but still. I stood alone in the living room; it was cold. The living room was always cold in the morning. I knew the paintings and ornaments that resided in there so well. Virtually unchanged since I was a young boy. Seen by me almost every day of my life till that point. They would only change their appearance with the changing time of day, the annual grind of the seasons or the rare broken bulb. I moved from there into the dining room. I could hear my mother in the kitchen already working through the breakfast dishes. The dining room was seldom used. Saved for special occasions such as Christmas or birthdays of significance. Eighteen Christmas dinners had been held in that room; eighteen times the family had been together and wished ourselves well. Some happy memories. I went up the stairs and back into my room. The final room I absolutely needed to see again before my departure. I sat on my bed and stared at the floor. I imagined being able to watch myself laying down on the floor as a little boy playing with toy cars and action figures, building impossible spaceships out of Lego. I had spent a lot of time alone in that room. I had many happy memories of amusing myself with toys and games. I wondered if I would view this house differently through student eyes. Would it appear somehow alternate through the eyes of a partially formed adult instead of a post-pubescent boy? I would find out. I let out a short sigh and looked at my clock. 07:55.

"Peter!" came the rattling wail of mother's voice up the stairs.

"Coming!" I called back loudly without shouting. Leaving my room, I shut the door behind me and heard that reassuring click of it closing tight. I thought that everyone who had ever had a bedroom of their own must instinctively know and recognise the sound of their own door closing. Like a kind of reassuring nightly therapy before getting into bed. Maybe not everyone, but I sure did. I marched down the stairs and was greeted by Mother and Father standing together next to the front door in anticipation of the final farewells. Mother wrapped her arms around me in a truly maternal embrace. As she let me go, my father extended his right arm to shake my hand. His grip was firm and strong, much stronger than mine. Stronger than most other 66-year-old men I'd have bet. Perhaps all children perceive their fathers to be stronger than they actually are? Perhaps.

"Good luck Peter," he stated.

But what I could hear him actually saying was, *"Don't let us down, Peter."* He continued.

"Make sure you ring us when you get there or you will have us both worried."

Again, what he was actually saying was, *"Make sure you ring us when you get there or you will have your mother worried and I will have to put up with her fretting."*

Father had never worried about me. He never worried if I was out late or staying somewhere away from home on something like a school trip. It wasn't because he didn't care. He just knew that whatever was going to happen was going to happen whether he worried about it or not. So he made the rational and logical decision to just not worry. To that date I hadn't ever done anything stupid or got hurt doing anything so his decision seemed to be vindicated.

"I will ring as soon as I get parked up in Llantarn, I promise."

"Well, just see that you do," said Mother in an unusually croaky tone.

With the hugs and handshakes concluded, I exited through the front door that I knew so well and strolled to my car on the drive. I opened the driver's side door and turned to see both my parents waving at me through the downstairs hall window. As I embarked, I thought I could make out my mother's face getting a little red and puffy, as if she were fighting back maternal tears that would not make a full appearance whilst I could still see her. I turned the key and the engine burst into life. Along with the engine the car radio also came to life. I turned it down a touch as it was always too loud when I started the car up. *"Why don't I ever turn this bloody thing down before I turn the engine off!"* I thought to myself. My parents were still stood by the window awaiting my departure. With the volume turned down I programmed the postcode into my satnav and put the car into reverse. I exited the drive without incident. I gave a barely visible wave at the direction of the hall window, put the car into first and that was it. The journey had begun. I checked the time on the car's clock: 08:01. *"Great,"* I thought, *"I'm late."*

09:00. Hit bad traffic going past Carlisle.

12:22. I stopped for a break. Apart from the Scottish B-roads it had been non-stop motorway since I'd left home. My eyes had become a little heavy with the hypnotic trance of white lines on dark tar. The recursive sequence of seemingly endless dashes, dots and conveyor belt service stations had started to get to me. I'd never driven for over an hour before in my life. I'd never had to. But now my fatigue had forced me into one of the factory produced flat-pack service stops that littered the roadway. I didn't need to use the buildings, I just wanted to borrow a car parking space for a bit so I could get out and stretch my legs before tucking in to some of the cheese and ham rolls my mother had prepared for me. She had given me four for the trip as well as a large bottle of still mineral water. After I had one of them, I thought about saving the rest, then I ate the other three. I was a growing lad after all. I felt like a full lad after I had devoured all four.

The weather was grey, overcast but warm enough for a September's day. I hadn't really done any proper motorway driving before that trip and didn't feel confident enough to spark up a cigarette behind the wheel with three lanes of madness constantly changing around me. So, I grabbed my smokes and the water and got out of the car to get some air. I walked slowly around the car and drank from the bottle. I mused to myself in an inner monologue about just turning around and going home.

"Turn back, go home, and do what? Get a job in a shop somewhere if you're lucky. Work for minimum wage, get condescended to by retarded customers and totalitarian management staff alike. Get a crap flat somewhere surrounded by morons and live on a diet of chips and 'own brand' lager. Would I convince myself that it was all worth it so I could save up for that one package holiday to Spain every year? Maybe I'd be willing to put myself through it if I had the love of a good woman, but probably not as I'd be far too selfish for something as limiting as that."

Before I knew it, I'd pondered away most of my cigarette. I didn't have a fully conscious memory of bringing it to my lips at any time but I felt like I had smoked it. I had another just to make sure. That time I switched off my inner voice, leant on my bonnet and just watched the cars zoom by. With my nicotine receptors sated for the time being I got back in the car and started the warm engine again. I drove off and hesitantly tried to nose back onto the hellishly busy motorway, waiting for a gap I could make or a generous road patron to let me on. After a minute or two waiting at the end of the slip road there was a gap and I and went for it. I made it. I felt renewed in my adventure with a full stomach, full lungs and loose legs. I leant over and turned the volume up on the dashboard. A bit of Oasis gave me an element of driving swagger, I pulled into the fast lane. My car's clock read 12:50.

Jesus Christ! The Welsh B-roads were just as bad as the Scottish ones, but I didn't know the Welsh ones like the back of my hand. I had clearly crossed the border at some point and just missed the big sign. Now all the signs were bi-lingual. Another sharp turn down another valley. It was a good job I never got travel sick as well as homesick. It had been nearly two hours since I had turned off the dual carriageway and the satnav proclaimed I still had forty minutes to go. I had no idea what the time was, no brain power to spend on a glance at the clock. I needed all my grey cells to focus on the driving, to focus on arriving at my destination alive without becoming a crash statistic.

Forty minutes later the satnav stated that there was still fifteen minutes to go. The roads had improved in quality if not width and isolation. I had relaxed a little. Then I tensed. A real nervous tension that I felt rise up inside me.

"Oh God" I thought, *"This is actually happening. I'm nearly there."*

Twenty minutes after that I passed into the town itself. I could remember parts of it from what I recalled of the Open Day. The time on the town clock read something near Three-forty-five. I saw the sign I drove all this way for…

'Croeso Llantarn'

'Welcome to Llantarn'

{Chapter 5}

|Till the first sleep|

The town was easy to navigate by road. It only had about three main streets. A swift double left turn took me straight into the main university car park. There were plenty of empty spaces so I parked up, turned the key and the car shuddered into stillness. The quick mechanised shunt as the car stopped sent ripples through my body. I almost felt like I was still in motion. But I was not. I was there, the journey was complete. I thought, *"Must ring home,"* so I picked up my mobile and rang the house. Mother answered.

"Hello?"

"Hi there, it's only me, I'm here safe and sound so no need to worry." I knew that would make her feel relieved and by extension my father too.

"Oh that's good son. Did you stop off and eat your rolls?" Mother asked, wanting to be reassured that I hadn't starved to death since leaving the house.

"Yes mother," I replied drolly.

"Did you hit any traffic?" she asked, no doubt primed by my father.

"No no, not at all," I lied, so as not to give my father any due satisfaction. Mother carried on,

"Have you got your room yet? Met any people? Not smoking are you?" Each question was asked before the previous could be answered. I really didn't need the barrage.

"No, no and no," I replied in stichomythic rhythm.

"Right then son, you had better go and get yourself sorted."

"Okay, will do." I couldn't wait to get off the phone and start sorting my life out.

"Right son, you go and get things sorted out. And don't be smoking!"

"Righty ho, speak to you later on, bye-bye." That was that; I hung up the phone and reached for my pack of cigarettes. It was time to leave the sanctuary of the car and I wasn't going to do that without a smoke. The uncertainty of what would come next was exhilarating. I opened the car door and was struck by the crisp scent of Welsh grass on the light air. It reminded me of Wordsworth, of the "*Blessing in this gentle breeze;*" it was beautiful. I felt secure and at ease despite all the excitement. I felt a physical warmth stir inside me. I felt as though no harm could come to me. I felt that I was home. It was bizarre, but I was more at home at the end of the journey than I had been at the start.

Finding the registration building was straightforward. Having already had a decent orientation of the campus from my quality Open Day experience, combined with the paper map I'd been sent as part of my joining pack, it made the task simple. In addition to that, there were large arrowed yellow and black signs labelled 'Registration' placed at strategic points around the campus. No doubt they would be of great help to students and parents who hadn't bothered to visit the place before applying. I supposed for some of them, maybe most of them, that Llantarn had been a second or even third choice for them to study at. Maybe Mr. Russett had even called here in an attempt to get Daz a place. That thought made me chuckle briefly to myself.

Before long I was at the final sign which read, 'Registration here, Old Hall Building', also displayed in incomprehensible Welsh. A minute or so later I was inside and waiting patiently in the line to register for accommodation in order to get my room issued. I was surrounded on all sides by scores of my fellow first years. Some I assumed were mature students due to their obvious ages; most though had young fresh faces similar to mine. Some of them looked like frightened ten-year-olds! The mature students appeared quite irritated at having to queue. I didn't see why they should be more irritated than anyone else. They must have had years more experience in queuing. The parents accompanying their student-children shared similar faces of irritation. I couldn't have imagined a worse hell than having had my parents come down here and be with me through it all. What a nightmare!

"Next," came a command in my direction. I stepped forward to present my papers. I knew everything was in order. The plethora of paperwork I handed over made sense to the thirty-something woman sat behind the desk. She stated, "This is your accommodation key," and she held it up unceremoniously. "Do try not to lose it. Academic registration is from twelve till three tomorrow back in here." Before I could say 'Thank you', I was herded away from the desk by a 'helper student' who went by the name of 'Jay'. He had long matted hair and questionable personal hygiene.

"Hey man, looks like you're in Hawson Hall," he mumbled to me as though I was supposed to know where he was talking about. All I could muster in response was a cheap, "Okay." He led on and implored, "Just follow me, it's not far." That statement made me grateful as the Old Hall Building was close to the Students' Union bar and so if I wasn't far from here, then I wasn't going to be far from there. As I set off half a pace behind my crusty guide, I heard the woman at the desk yell out again, "Next."

My room. The door had a small metallic '58' screwed into it. I found that mildly perplexing as it was the first room on the left of the ground floor. I would have asked Jay about it but as soon as he had shown me the door he just turned about and quietly spat, "Any issues please report them to the accommodation office. Have a good one man." And he was gone. So, I inserted the key into the lock, turned it and entered. It was not a large room. It was, in fact, bloody tiny. It was not the type of room I had stayed in when I had visited for the Open Day. Not one of the fancy en-suite rooms that was pictured in the university's prospectus. Its contents were: one very single bed with bedside table and lamp, one built in wardrobe, a sink with mirror screwed to the wall, a desk and chair, and a floating bookcase firmly secured to the wall. The walls consisted of a breeze block lattice which had, once upon a time, been painted white. At least I had a window. Its curtains bore the hue of nicotine yellow stains and were in dire need of replacement. This room was to be where I would spend a whole year of my life. It was a shit hole, and I loved it! It was mine and that was all that mattered. My mother wasn't going to be bursting through the door at any time of day or night to put washing away. It was a blank canvas. It was *my* blank canvas. I actually had a space that was really mine. I mean I obviously didn't own the place, but it was as close to mine as I had ever known. For the first time in my life I actually felt like I had some of my own leg space. I was exhilarated - I needed to smoke. I knew from my experiences at the Open Day that none of the fire alarms in the accommodation were sensitive to cigarette smoke. I'd been in a room somewhere in a block with nigh on ten other people all smoking simultaneously and that hadn't set it off. But my room was bereft of a key piece of furniture: an ashtray. Until one was acquired, I would smoke outside. I exited the main door of my new accommodation hall and I saw a premium location to sit and smoke. An old metal bike hut. I sat on it and let the early evening sun kiss my brow as I brought the flickering flame to my face to light my cigarette. With the first inhalation I thought about the unfortunate logistics which came with my situation. I had to shuttle my belongings from the car into my new residence. I hadn't brought much so I was sure I could complete that task within the hour. As I smoked, I saw an intermittent raft of other people walking in and out of Hawson, most with parents in tow. I was so glad to be free of that pressure. I exhaled the freedom away in a cloud of grey. Soon I would get to know the people I'd be living with, but not just yet. As I extinguished my cigarette, I contemplated my next move. The car would be my destination. I supposed that two trips would be all that would be required to bring all of my gear to my room. Once it was in my room, I'd be able to unpack and settle in. Once everything was in its place, I'd be able to really relax. And by 'really relax', I meant get upside-down drunk.

Three round trips to the car later I had successfully emptied my belongings into my room. I had taken the extra trip to bring the new laptop and a selection of the liberated CDs from the car. My room was a small place so I was even more glad I had packed reasonably light. My corridor had six other student rooms and we were all to share one kitchen and one toilet/shower facility. I could hear multiple rumblings from other rooms along the corridor and upstairs. No doubt there were people in a frenzied buzz about moving in just the same as me. Amongst the ongoing background noise, I unzipped my suitcase and began the unpacking process. I'd just about completed the act of placing one pair of socks away into my wardrobe when a knock planted on my door. I opened the door to be met with the sight of a thin male with greasy hair just past shoulder length. This was all the more bizarre because it seemed to be combined with a mid-stage receding hairline. He sported a mesh of ratty facial hair and wore a kaleidoscopic coloured t-shirt fused with ripped stonewash denim jeans and a pair of old navy converse trainers.

"Heya pal, I'm Steve, but call me Ste," he said, revealing a slow-soft Glaswegian accent.

"Hello Ste, I'm Pete," I replied revealing my extraordinarily soft and middle-class Scottish Borders accent. In fact, I was sure he just thought I was English. He didn't seem to regard my accent in any way and continued with the reason he had knocked.

"Av go a crate a lager in ma room. Fancy crackin' it open and getting' a chat on eh?"

"Aye," I replied, trying to make my own Scottish heritage clear. "Sounds great," I added. I had rolled the R in the 'great' just a touch to reinforce the Scottish camaraderie. I didn't know why I had done that. Perhaps it was just a normal social mirror I was trying to hold up. Perhaps I just wanted to put out a friendly flag to indicate some Celtic unity.

"I'm just doon here at the end on the left pal," he gestured pointing down the corridor towards his room. Having nothing to lose I just followed him there and before I knew it, I had a drink in my hand. Then another, and another. The following twelve hours or so were a blur. I was sure other people had arrived in his room. I was certain there had been more lager. Other than that, I was pretty lost in a mind-haze.

My next solid memory was of giving up trying to work out how to take my shoes off before getting into my bed. I looked at my watch and it said - it said, something or other. In that inebriated state, I just lay back and let sleep claim me. Whatever had happened was no doubt good and fun. The first night of many I was sure. I allowed my eyes to close and the drunken slumber took me. My final thought that night was, *"I like it here."*

{Chapter 6}

|Fully Fledged Student|

I woke up and realised that I was fully dressed. I sat up on the edge of my bed and felt slightly sick. I could have felt worse. Clearly my youth had worked to keep the main body of the hangover at bay. I hadn't closed my curtains before passing out which led to the morning sunlight streaming through the window to nurse me awake. I stretched up and saw the time. It was exactly nine o'clock. I took off my shoes as well as all my clothes and rose off the mattress. It was time for a shower. A shower would help sort me out. I scuffled around in my suitcase to find my washbag so I could get my shower gel. I withdrew a pair of red and navy flip-flops which I donned. I also pulled out my big towel and wrapped it around my waist before venturing to the shower room at the end of the corridor. My flip-flops produced a light strike against the old red linoleum floor.

In the shower I felt my body rejuvenate as the warm water struck my skin and washed over me. The water wasn't at the high pressure I had come to expect from the shower at my parents' house, but it would suffice. Stepping out of the cubicle I felt clean – fresh, even. On the way back to my room the wet flip-flops made a pronounced slap against the floor that echoed all the way down the corridor and back again. Upon returning to my room I was faced with a still-packed suitcase and rucksack. I would have to perform an unorganised dig to find clothes to wear. After some tossing about, I had a t-shirt and some pants. Fortunately, I knew exactly where to find some socks as I had at least put one pair away in the wardrobe. I was up and about, ready to attack the day. I had a few hours to kill before academic registration. What would I do? I decided against unpacking as I didn't want to upset anyone's morning by slamming drawers and cupboard doors.

After a highly pleasant morning stroll around the campus site which took in some of the adjoining hills and fields, I found myself in the centre of Llantarn town itself. I noticed a small quiet-looking café and decided to head in for a pot of tea and some toast. The premises had a no smoking policy, but you couldn't win them all. The tea was so, so, nice. No better word for it. Not nice in the polite sense, nice in the extraordinarily meaningful way of being simply rather lovely. I couldn't stay there too long because of the smoking policy so after I paid up and left, I headed for the academic registration. I had to go via my room first to pick up the papers before what would be, no doubt, another queue. The plan was simple: get registered then unpack properly. There was plenty of time.

The registration event gave me the opportunity to observe my now parentless student peers. It gave them the chance to observe me too. I was exactly on time for the registration which had somehow put me at the back of the line. It was an ideal place to look at the people in front of me. What a sight! I had never seen the likes before in such magnitude: the people seemed semi-alien. My conservative rural upbringing in the backwaters of Scotland had in no way prepared me for such a level of vivid diversity. There was a gaggle of dreadlocks, tattoos, piercings, checked shirts, long hair, longer hair, no hair. Shades, hats of all kinds, luminous shoes, black nail varnish, and pink lace under large buckled boots. I had previously only seen the variation of people on display in front of me on TV shows or comic books. They were my peers. They were the people I would be spending my academic and social time with. I couldn't wait. One way or another I was sure it would be interesting. I had seen a few people dressed along those lines when I was at the Open Day, but the sheer concentration of them was certainly a scene to behold. Clearly Llantarn was a refugee camp for the defunct and lonely souls of my generation. I was glad they were there. I was glad they had Llantarn to retreat to: nature's academic asylum would welcome them with open arms and open hearts.

Finally, I was at the front of the queue.

"Next," came the call. Unlike the woman of the previous day this voice was male, old and deep. I stepped up to the desk and got a clear look at him. He resembled Doc Brown from 'Back to the Future'. He spoke again,

"OK, this all seems to be in order." He tapped my papers down like a veteran newsreader.

"Right," he proceeded to say. "Please tick next to the modules you want to study this year."

I was slightly taken aback. I hadn't realised that the process of deciding the exact classes you wanted to study was as perfunctory. I managed to force out a reply.

"Erm, okay." I was conscious of the people waiting in order behind me. I rapidly ran my eyes over the list presented to me. Metaphysics, Epistemology, Ethics, Early Greek, Continental, Oriental, Philosophy of Religion, Introduction to Political Philosophy. That was my list. I had to pick five out of the eight to study. I had done no real research into what these sub-topics were. I had absolutely no idea what 'Metaphysics' or 'Epistemology' were. Naturally I selected both of them. The thought of being able to logically argue with my mother about her faith made me tick 'Philosophy of Religion'. I was more than half-way done, three out of five. I had heard the names Plato, Socrates and Pythagoras banded around in my life however I had no real idea who they were or what they stood for, so I ticked again on 'Early Greek Philosophy'. If I was going to learn about one ancient philosophy I might as well learn about another, so my final tick went next to 'Oriental Philosophy'. And it was done. I had selected what in my most uninformed opinion would give me a pretty well-rounded foundation in Philosophy. Handing back my form I asked, "Is that it?"

"That's it," came his reply. After a few seconds he glanced back up at me from his papers with a sort of *"Why are you still here?"* expression on his face. I saw the look for what it was and shuffled off to one side. That was another vital task completed, the time was right to unpack back in my room. I left the Old Hall Building and sparked up a smoke as soon as I did. I started back to Hawson Hall and as I did

I passed many people still queuing up to register. I felt an unwarranted feeling of mock superiority as I had already completed it and was free from the queue. I walked back to my room, puffing every step of the way.

Upon returning to my corridor I could hear a hustle coming from the communal kitchen. I thought for a moment about entering but thought again. I needed to sort my room out and all I would need was a couple of hours to do it. Though I was sure that however I'd arrange my room, it wouldn't be up to my mother's standard. She was definitely placed on the OCD spectrum. I entered my room and set to work.

Sitting down on the end of my crisply made bed I felt a modicum of pride. The room was done. The few books I'd brought with me were neatly lined up on the shelf along with the digital travel clock my mother had provided me. All the clothes were firmly folded and pressed away into the provided storage. There was just enough space between the end of the desk and the wall to slot my guitar into. My wash bag was emptied around my sink into the most functional order I could compose. The new laptop was centre-stage on the desk and looked like the carpenter's tool awaiting the artisan. I sat down at the desk and fingered my way through the last multi-coloured pile of papers I still had to hand in.

My final appointment was at the Students' Union administration building the following day. That would be for registering with the National Union of Students and would result in me getting my student card. Again, it was between noon and three o'clock. The day after that would be the Freshers' Fair located in the New Hall, then a few days after that, the Freshers' Ball would officially christen Freshers' Week. One of the pieces of paper I had in my hands was the flyer for the ball. The timing simply read, '7 till late'. I wondered what 'late' meant down here. I'd find out. I would be there to see it for myself. Amid my rustlings of paper, I became increasingly aware of the noise that was still being projected out of the kitchen. The hullabaloo had been rising up steadily for the entire time I had been arranging my room. It was hard to ignore as the shared kitchen was immediately opposite my room. Sound travelled pretty well in the building. I had been waiting for my door to be knocked on but it hadn't been. I was grateful for the lack of interruption. It allowed me to work on my own to do what needed to be done. But now those jobs were complete I fancied a drink. I decided that I would go straight in and join them. I was sure I must have met some of them the previous night and no doubt said or done something stupid and/or funny that they'd remember. I hoped I hadn't done anything that had inadvertently seriously offended them. I hoped that that wasn't the reason they hadn't knocked on my door to invite me in. There was no point in worrying about that; I'd just go in and face the music. I'd apologise if necessary.

I left my room and heard the music in the kitchen as it became louder and clearer. Led Zeppelin, nice. I strode the one pace to the kitchen door and bravely entered. As I pressed hard to open the kitchen door the music shot up in volume and clarity without the door to attenuate the sound. There were half a dozen young male bodies in there. As the door closed behind me, I had a dozen eyes trained on me. I felt somewhat in the spotlight. I was sure that most people would have done in that circumstance. The room was heavy with hazed layers of smoke; a large speaker blared in the corner and green beer bottles covered every surface - some were empty but most were still full with lids on. A couple of the faces seemed vaguely familiar, no doubt from last night. I couldn't remember their names. But I could remember the name of the guy sat at the table wearing the same bright t-shirt he wore the previous day. My Glaswegian host from last night. He reached over to the speaker to turn the volume down a touch. I tried to take the initiative and introduce myself but Ste beat me to it.

"Pete!" He yelled in a tipsy stupor that I was instantly jealous of. "Bout time ye got ya'sell in here man." He stood up and handed me a full green bottle. I held my hand out and welcomed it gladly. I hesitated, then spoke,

"Um, hey everyone. I'm Pete, as you might have gathered. I am sure I met some of you last night but I can't remember any of your names." I thought honesty would be the best policy. One of the guys sat around the table spoke up in reply,

"Oh not to worry mate, none of us remember a thing either. That's why we are having this kitchen sesh so we can hopefully all meet again properly. I'm Dave, but we'll probably have all forgotten again by tomorrow so who cares." He spoke with a mumbling scouse accent but confusingly wore a Welsh football shirt. I was sure I'd get the story behind that at some point. Ste stood up and took the lead.

"Well, now that Pete's here, I'd like us all te stand and huv a toast." Everyone obliged him and he carried on: "Te corridor number wan of Hawson Hawl!" All raised their bottles and chanted in unison, "Corridor number one of Hawson Hall!" A series of jubilant screams, cheers and hoots flowed from all including me. Suddenly I thought of a nice little word play that I just couldn't keep to myself. Boosted by the confidence and pregnant friendship in the room I yelled out, "To corridor number one of Hawson Hall, the Whore Sons!"

The rest of them just looked at each other, then right back at me. Huge grins decorated all of their faces. I took a punt and led the new, more succinct toast, "The Whore Sons!"

"THE WHORE SONS!" came the raucous response from all, glasses raised again.

Energy from youthful lungs lit up the room's atmosphere. I felt good; I felt outstanding. After the howls, a drinking riot commenced. Seven people had started to bond, had started to forge a team identity of alcohol and friendship and shared nicknames. By the end of the night I knew everyone's name and they all knew mine.

When I woke the next day, I could remember Ste and Dave, but that was it. *"Oh well,"* I thought, *"Two is better than one!"* I had things to do. Fortunately the morning's hangover was again kept in check by my youth, though I had felt the lag of lethargy pull at me. The clock read 12:01. "Bollocks!" I yelled out loud. I imagined the size of the queue to get my student card. It looked rather long in my mind. I decided on an alternative strategy. Instead of getting there as quickly as I could I would turn up at around five to three. That way there'd just be some stragglers left and the endless queue would be avoided. I still got out of bed though as I wanted a shower. I grabbed my towel, slipped on my flip flops and as I opened my door to venture down the corridor to the wet room I was assaulted by the odour of spilt lager and stale cigarette smoke. I exhaled hard with puffed-out cheeks, but even my youth was unable to prevent a small retch. It was just a small one though, and with that small convulsion put to bed I went and had my shower.

A few cleansing minutes later I was back in my room drying off. I was hungry. I wanted food. I would have loved Mother to come in and put a fry-up down in front of me, but that wasn't going to happen. I would get dressed and take a voyage into town and find a greasy spoon of some sort. The Freshers' handbook had an advert for some place called 'Wynn's Diner'. The accompanying photograph made it look like a good place to try. I got dressed, got my shoes on and left my room. I locked the door and stopped myself for a moment to have a quick listen. I couldn't hear a sound. I supposed I was the only one up in the corridor - or the rest of them were in the queue. I decided it best not to go knocking on anyone's doors to invite them along as they probably wouldn't appreciate the wakeup call. I left Hawson and headed into town.

The greasy plateful I stuffed down at 'Wynn's Diner' sorted me right out. It had chased away any ill effects from last night's binge and replaced it with a warm, wholesome feeling. With my stomach full I leant back in my chair and lit up a fresh cigarette from a new packet. As I smoked, I gently sipped my tea and felt supremely content with myself and with the world. In front of me, beside my empty plate I had a copy of the newspaper that I had flicked through whilst waiting for my order to come to fruition. With the food gone I took up where I had left off. I felt so grown up. I felt that by doing such things it would cast off the shell of 'Pete the boy', and usher in 'Pete the man'. After getting to the back pages I placed the paper down and turned my gaze outside. I didn't look at anything in particular, I just fell into a sort of trance. A helpless daydream. The autumn sun was stroking the skin of my bare forearms through the glass. I was by no means the only customer. There were random pairs of terribly dressed students dotted about. I imagined conversations about politics and Doctor Who going on between them. It made me laugh inside. There were also some elderly locals sat with pots of tea and rounds of toast chatting away in fluent Welsh. There didn't seem to be any animosity towards the students from the townspeople. The university had been around for hundreds of years so they must have been used to it all by now; must have grown up seeing a constant stream of oddly dressed undernourished young people.

My thoughts drifted onto the topic of how lucky I was. I was eighteen years old, fit, well and physically healthy. Free from all disease and disability. I had been born into a privileged family in a wealthy nation. I was at an academic institute that was going to teach me things that I wanted to learn. I had limitless borders, countless boundaries, an open horizon of life to explore. I took one last puff and put my cigarette out. The time shown on the wall clock was 14:30. It's funny how you can phase out of time when left to dance in your own thoughts. I paid for the food and left with purpose. It was time to officially become a student.

Ten minutes later, I was standing in what remained of the queue for my official student registry. Just as I had thought, only a couple of stragglers. My turn came quickly and within a blur of papers and something involving a digital camera and a laminating machine I was back outside. In my hand I had the still-warm proof that I was in fact a student. I looked down at it with pride. 'Peter Morgan – National Union of Students'. It was a poor photo of me but that didn't matter. I felt like a real student, I was a real student. A real member of the university. The priority at the time was clear: smoke a cigarette as a student for the first time.

{Chapter 7}

|Freshers' Fair|

It was a mix of colourful sights. The Freshers' Fair had been assembled in the New Hall. By the time I arrived it was a teeming hive of vibrant activity. I walked in slowly in an effort to take it all in. Flyers were being thrust in every direction; demonstrations of activities were being performed to clustered pockets of students. A group of guys that looked like extras from 'Enter the Dragon' were all dressed up going through some sort of routine whilst one of them broke a piece of wood with his foot. The purpose of the fair was to display all of the clubs and societies of the university in the hopes that keen young freshers would sign up and join whichever one took their fancy. Everyone, from the military reserve to the horticultural society were there to do their best to ensnare new members. They all wanted signatures and deposits and all claimed to be amazing. The fact was that if any society dropped to below ten members then it wouldn't qualify for any university funding. Each of the clubs was lobbying for their own existence. Some of them did look quite fun though. The circus society put on a great show of juggling, and fire staffs twirled with impressive flare. Not something I could see myself spending any time learning to do, but good to have watched nonetheless. Whilst strolling down the first row I was accosted by a six-foot-tall woman with short purple/grey dreadlocks. Before I knew it, her face was no more than six inches away from my nose as she spouted her rhetoric.

"Are you aware how much your body and mind would benefit from only eating fruit and vegetables that you'd grown yourself in a pesticide-free environment?" She asked it in a manner more in the style of a demand than a question. Before I could formulate an answer I had a beige pamphlet entitled 'Llantarn Home Organics Society' thrust into my hand. She simply instructed me to "Think about it!" and moved onto someone else who had walked in behind me. I tried to brush off the confrontational scene I'd just been a part of and continued on my way down the rows of desks.

I passed the rugby stand. It was dominated by large burly men who were wearing the uni team strip. They were no doubt on the hunt for muscular and athletic types. The type of guys Henrietta would have gone for. All muscles, tattoos, designer stubble and deep voices. I walked past them without comment. They'd have had no interest in my knitting needle arms and legs anyway so that was fine. I had been forced to play rugby regularly at Woodbourne as part of the 'character building' nature of the establishment. Unsurprising given the school's location in the Scottish Borders, the heart of Rugby Union's grass roots. However now I was delighted to be rid of the requirement to play. I had never been much of a sportsman. The only mildly physical activity I was relatively good at and actually enjoyed was swimming. There was no swimming society, due to the lack of a swimming pool within a thirty-mile radius. Sometimes whilst being sat alone in the sixth form common room at Woodbourne, I would reason that my lack of sporting prowess was one of the reasons I'd not been so popular. Or perhaps it was my propensity to be sarcastic and to talk shit. Probably both. Neither of them went down particularly well with my fellow pupils or faculty staff. But this wasn't Woodbourne, it was Llantarn. It wasn't school or college, it was university. The days of being a pupil had finished; the time of the student had arrived.

I walked aimlessly round till one station caught my eye. 'Unplugged Society' was an acoustic music club that met every Saturday for a couple of hours in one of the upstairs rooms inside the union building. It was through chatting with the guy on the stand that informed me of how the societies operated within the bar. Every academic year a club or society could book an evening in the union bar and basically take it over and put on a show. Naturally 'Unplugged Soc' were requested more regularly due to the nature of the society itself. I liked the sound of it all. I had brought my guitar so I might as well have a little jam and learn how to play a bit better. I handed over ten pounds and signed on the dotted line. I was moving up in the world; I was a student who was part of a university society. A shame really, as it would transpire, I would never play a single note with any of them. Anyway, I was exceedingly impressed with myself and decided to leave and go for a pint and a smoke. I thought I should go and check in with the 'Whore Sons' first and find out if there was a wider plan for the evening. I hadn't seen any of them all day.

I got back to the corridor and heard a similar sound to previous night's hustle emanating once again from the kitchen. I walked in to join it and was greeted by a group "AYYYY!" with smiles and laughs reverberating at all angles. "It's Pete!" shouted Dave. A beer was jousted into my palm along with chants of "Down it Pete ... down it Pete!" from the whole group. I didn't disappoint. About two hours later we had all managed to navigate our way down to the union bar. An almost endless string of sambucas stole the rest of that night from me.

{Chapter 8}
|Philosophy|

"What is Philosophy?" were the opening words of my first lecture as a student. In fact, it wasn't a proper lecture, it was a voluntary event: an open invitation for an introduction to the department and an overview of some of the subject matter that would be covered in the first year. It was delivered by Dr. Pathe. An Irishman in his late sixties. Small-statured and generally meek in appearance, but immensely respected by the faculty. It was he that would propel my mind into taking its first steps into the philosophy arena. He asked again: "What is Philosophy?"

There were about forty of us in the lecture hall and upon the second time the question was posed we realised that it wasn't a rhetorical introductory statement, it was a real question. Despite that realisation still nobody spoke. Everyone just shuffled slightly and looked around.

"Well, anyone?" Dr. Pathe pushed. A hand tentatively broke head level to offer an answer. The offer was accepted.

"You with your hand in the air, stand up so we can all see you." I thought to myself, *"Jesus, this is worse than GCSE History with Mr. Demptham"*. The thought came with an accompanying flashback to his lessons at Woodbourne. Row upon row of children stood on tables, unable to return to their seats until they had answered at least five questions correctly. Each question pertaining to the pre-reading homework that had been set out during the last lesson. I could remember being the last boy standing on more than one occasion. It wasn't a nice feeling, and that was amongst a group of people I already knew! I would have hated to be standing in front of all these new peers with the academic spotlight on me straight away. Dr. Pathe pressed again.

"Introduce yourself to everyone and present an answer." Dr. Pathe's tone was direct but not interrogative. His soft Irish inflections removed any bite that may have dwelt in his words. He got his answer.

"Hey guys. My name is Reece, and to answer the question, I think that Philosophy is about trying to equate and combine ideologies with practical application in real life." Reece sounded like he'd sat next to Prince William throughout his school career. He was tall, well-groomed and extraordinarily well-spoken. A typical buffoon type. He concluded his answer with an excessively smug grin. I didn't like him. He was the epitome of public-school boy. I mean, I had been privately schooled too but this just took the piss. He had at least put his hand up. I hadn't. Dr. Pathe answered him expansively.

"Oh, okay Reece. Thanks very much, but the question was a bit more literal than that." After a pause lasting several seconds longer than it should have Reece was still standing. "Feel free to sit down now," suggested Dr. Pathe. Reece sat down still grinning. Dr. Pathe went over to one of the wheeled chalk boards and dragged it front and centre. He wrote two words. "PHILO" and "SOPHY." He then explained.

"PHILO, from the ancient Greek meaning love. SOPHY, likewise from ancient Greek, meaning wisdom. Put them together and we have 'The love of wisdom'." He placed the chalk down and started up again,

"That is why you are all here, or that is why you *should* all be here. You want to know things, not because it is good to know things, but because you *love* to know things. I also hope that all of you have questions that you struggle with personally. Questions you cannot answer. During your time here you will learn to properly scrutinise answers and the questions that spew them forth. Philosophy is a science. It is the science of thought. The methods are logical. But we won't be using computers and calculators. Ideas and propositions will be attacked with reasoned argument like any new scientific theory would be. For the wider sakes of your own lives I hope you are able to use these techniques to provide yourselves with any specific answers you came here hoping to find. If you do then you will have to come back here and teach us all about it. Now," he suggested as he took his seat, "Shall we begin?" We began.

About an hour later I was sat in the union bar nursing my first beer of the day. Quite late for my first drink being that it was nearly three 'o'clock. I was sat in one of the cosy corner areas with a small round table. I was organising my notes from Dr. Pathe's 'Introduction to Philosophy' session. I always wrote my notes by hand using a pencil. I loved the organic feel of it. It was like carving the words into the paper. It was also easy to rub out. I looked up from my wrinkly graphite-soaked papers and saw Ste and Tim making a beeline for me. Ste had had a change of clothes and he was clean shaven which surely must have meant he'd also had a shower. They both sat with me in the small alcove. Tim lived in the room opposite to Ste's; he was a plump Yorkshire lad who hailed from the city of Leeds. He'd often preach about it being "God's City on God's side'ut Pennines." He was possessed of large, unkempt curly dark hair and a seemingly endless supply of rolling tobacco. I had only known him a few days but I liked him a lot - though his friendly demeanour had the tendency to be offset by his recurring negativity about absolutely everything. He had been present for the second night in Hawson kitchen and all that came with that. As he sat, he looked at my papers quizzically.

"What ya up to then lad?" came his deep and overwhelmingly chirpy voice.

"Philosophy Dep held a welcome lecture. Just an overview of what all the various topics and sub-topics consists of and what we can expect from the next year and beyond. It was pretty interesting. I'm just sorting out the notes I took." I clicked my notes into place in a folder and stowed the folder into my bag. It got the precious papers away from any possible beer spillage and created room for Ste and Tim to put their drinks down properly. I continued aloud on my train of thought.

"Think it was a good opportunity for the teachers…"
I stopped myself mid-sentence realising what a stupid
school-boy error I'd just made. I thought I had made such
a huge fool of myself. "I'm sorry, lecturers," came out like
a cup of cold sick. Ste and Tim didn't seem to care in the
slightest. If I had made a similar slip of the tongue back in
the sixth form common room there would have been jeers
and chants for days. Here there was none of that. I inhaled
and started again.

"I think it was just a good opportunity to get an
explanation of some of the terminology so when we try
writing something, we don't freak out too badly." I lit a
cigarette as soon as I finished my sentence. My pint glass
was still half full, so I would be out of synchronisation
with the other two for the round. I was sure we'd work it
out somehow. Ste looked deep in thought and hadn't
spoken a word since he'd sat down. He drew his pint to his
lips and drank half of it in one. He placed his glass down
and asked,

"So, Pete, what exactly is Philosophy anyway?"

I tapped some residual ash from the end of my cigarette
into the ashtray, leant backwards and inhaled. I exhaled a
beautiful stream of smoke and began.

"Well, Philosophy is…

{Chapter 9}
|The Ball|

The next day was the day of the Freshers' Ball. The end of a week of induction into life as a student. The ball was the peak of the week. As I understood, it was a huge party in which every student on campus would get steaming drunk. There would be shots. There would be vomit. Then the challenge to find a partner to take back to your room for extra-curricular, non-committal activities. Sounded like a blast! Since my arrival I had been persistently successful at the drinking element, however I had yet to ensnare one of the young campus damsels for debauchery. I was by no means a virgin. At that time I already had six notches on my bed post. Not that that was a particularly obscene number for an eighteen-year-old male in the western world, but enough to feel a certain level of confidence that I at least had some idea about how things operated in that regard. Even though I hadn't been popular at school I knew that I wasn't unpopular enough for parties to turn me away, especially when I brought good quality booze and cigarettes. Teenage parties had been my avenue for female exploration. Besides, there were always some less than popular girls at parties too. I'd had some pretty positive experiences, though woefully never with Henrietta. She would at least come over and initiate conversations with me. Whether she was genuinely interested in talking to me or just raising my social stock by proxy I didn't know. I didn't much care either. Time with her was good time. All in all, I'd had enough experience to know what I liked and what I didn't. At the ball, I wanted to find something I liked.

At six o'clock our Hawson kitchen was on the upper end of lively. I could hear the familiar buzz emanating through the wall. The drinking had clearly begun in earnest. I was not long out of the shower. All cleaned up and ready for the evening. I dried off, cleaned out my ears with baby buds, ran a neat toothcomb through my hair and applied shaving foam to my face. I stood in front of the mirror above my sink and began to remove my few facial whiskers. The popular blues sound of Pink Floyd blared away from my laptop speakers and I could feel myself sway at the hips to the rhythm. I felt good. Shave complete I rubbed on some face cream and slipped into my shirt for the night. A white crushed velvet number with a thorny black pattern racing down one side. Pants and socks on. The trusty black jeans were next, sporting my 'Marlboro Classic' belt buckle. I gave myself an extended spray of deodorant and used my wet-look gel to spike up my hair. I was ready. I made a decision. I would call home as I had had several missed calls in the last couple of days. Mother was probably worried so I thought I would alleviate the concern and put her mind at rest. I picked up the phone and dialled.

"Hello, it's only me," I led with. I wanted to get into the kitchen and join the drinking and laughing. I would try and make it short and sweet.

"Hello there son, how are you doing?" she asked with tension. I answered with positivity and optimism in my voice,

"I'm fine thanks, really great. I'm-" Mother cut me off.

"You sound throaty, are you smoking all the time?" I was so glad that I had called!

"No, no, not at all. Must just be the line." I was about ready to end the call already. I probably did sound a little hoarse in truth. Everyone in the corridor smoked. That's because everyone in my corridor had selected the 'smoking' box on the accommodation paperwork. That was the real reason we were all in the decrepit accommodation. They weren't listed as specific smoking halls, but we had eyes and could join the dots together. It didn't matter where we smoked inside Hawson. Bedroom, bathroom, kitchen or corridor. No alarms ever went off.

"Peter, are you eating properly like I told you to?" she rolled on.

"Yes of course. I made a huge pot of pasta today with lots of fresh vegetables that will keep me going for a few days at least." That was a lie, but she wouldn't have felt good about me telling her that I was going to Wynn's every day for fry-ups. Mother started to speak again but my interest was so low I couldn't maintain positivity any longer. "Oh sorry. Battery is dying. Going to have to go and plug it in."

"Oh, okay son, you go and plug it in. Take care of yourself and don't be acting like a fool with the drink."

"Love you." I forced out.

"Love you too son. Bye-bye." As soon as she bade her farewell and the line was dead I breathed a sigh of relief. It was done. She would feel better because I had made contact and declared my safety and sensibility. It was past time I was in the kitchen.

I bounced through the kitchen door. I was the last member of the corridor to join the party and I had drinking time to make up. The sun was already retreating for the day and there was a dull low light illuminating the room. A lager was thrust into my hand from somewhere and it tasted like freedom. I knew everyone's face and name. Ste, Dill, Tim, Wozza, Dave and Danny. All were dressed to impress. Even Ste had styled his hair. We all clinked bottles and smiled. We drank and laughed. I was actually liked; I was actually accepted. Listened to without prejudice. We were forging a unique cauldron that would hopefully last forever. Is this what being young was meant to feel like? A crucible of wit, smiles, care and understanding?

Several hours later, the corridor descended as a unit on the ball. At the bar I heard Dill order: "Eight pints and eight slammers please." He had to shout in his broad Northern Irish accent; the music filling the bar was oppressively loud. With shots in hand we counted down together, "Three, two, one!" The slammers vortexed their way down our gullets. We jerked our heads, claimed our pints and worked our way to a table just large enough for us all to cram on to. A short fat body brushed past me and we made passing eye contact. He spoke through a straggly beard.

"Pete, great to see you," came the unfamiliar voice.

"You too," I replied in confused politeness.

"I'm just going to the bar, will catch up later." He spoke loudly.

"Absolutely mate, no worries," was my cheerful reply. He vanished into the throng of bodies as we all sat down.

"Who was that?" asked Tim about two inches from my ear.

"Not a clue," was my honest response. Tim shrugged in acceptance and reached for one his pre-rolled cigarettes. I followed suit and reached for my smokes. Like a sympathetic action all seven of us sparked up and chained together, as if smoking was our corridor's uniform. The music shifted gear and became more dance orientated. We weren't thoroughly drunk yet. We just all felt relaxed and comfortable with each other and the surroundings. It wouldn't be long before the dance floor became infested with the beautiful young.

The night travelled onwards. Nightclub shouting matches that passed for conversations went on all around. It got to the point where I was so drunk that I saw the dance floor and couldn't help myself. I walked towards it and didn't look back. I was sure I would be admonished by the group for my action. I was too drunk to care. I just wanted to dance. After only seconds the rest of my corridor were right up on the dancefloor with me. We were all gyrating and shoulder rolling in our own way. I had led the group up here. It was inadvertent. I hadn't intended on making a leadership play. But I had gone, and they had followed. Nothing like that had ever happened to me before. I felt like a leader. It felt powerful. We all danced, we all drank. What a great night.

"Good morning," came a gentle voice from across the pillow. My eyes had not yet opened. My brain was certainly not yet engaged. Memories of the ball were like a sharp hidden dream. There was another body in my bed. A naked body. That was no dream. I pried my eyelids apart. I saw a pretty blonde girl next to me. She was by far the most attractive woman I had ever had in a bed before.

"Good morning," I managed to say with my head rested on the pillow, face to face with hers.

"Fancy going again?" she quizzed lightly. I had no idea who she was or what had taken place between us.

"Oh God yes," I quipped in a hushed, gleeful tone.

{Chapter 10}

|Beyond Physics|

It was the first full week of term and I had developed a sort of strut that I would subconsciously engage when walking around the campus - basically I'd walk around as if I owned the place. Socially I felt pretty settled; professionally I was ready to get stuck in. For my first formal lecture I was up well in advance; I was smartly dressed. My bag was primed with sheets of crisp blank paper and sharp pencils. I would surely arrive at the lecture room early. The full layout of the campus was exceedingly compact. You could walk it end to end in under quarter of an hour. There were no long marches to get to a class, yet every walk still felt like taking the scenic route. I was excited and nervous as I stepped out of Hawson and in to my future. My eyes swept all around as I took in the world. The trees blew with bowing grace and the grass wept with the morning dew. I wondered how many students the trees must have seen walking to and fro over the decades, over the centuries even. How many young bodies and minds had basked in the sunshine of bygone afternoons laid on the grass? Who could say?

On my way to the Philosophy Department I strolled past the Old Hall Building. The Hall where I had initially registered all that time ago. An entire week ago! Simultaneously the longest and shortest week of my life till then. I felt I had come so far as a person. It was transformative. I felt liberated. I felt older, yet I was still to properly start my development. Seven days of drinking, talking and being happy. I'd had fun, and the time had flown. Now was the time to work. The Philosophy Department's building was a crooked looking red brick structure adjacent to the Old Hall Building by about two hundred yards. It sat on the corner of a crossroads and looked like a red lattice of aged worn power. That was the place I would be for eight hours of lectures and four hours of tutorial seminars every week.

Ha! It would be tough doing a twelve-hour week, but I'd make it work.

I entered. Upon the murky walls were laminated signs with arrows that read, 'METAPHYSICS'. I dutifully followed the signs which led me up a narrow set of wooden stairs. I almost felt like I was scaling the innards of an old galleon, but the smell wasn't of salt water: it was of cold stone, seasoned timber and old books. The heady aroma reminded me of the main library back at Woodbourne. I revelled in it; it set me at ease. At the top of the stairs I followed another 'METAPHYSICS' pointer. It directed me to take a left and carry on till the end of the corridor. I walked into a room that had a small wooden sign stating 'First Year METAPHYSICS' hanging on a hook. The room was a basic rectangle with desks along each side. On the far wall was a large white board with some associated marker pens strewn around it. I wasn't the first to arrive. Two people sat next to each other at one of the desks at the far end. I sat down at the seat closest to the door. I unslung my bag and withdrew my virgin paper pads and my rapier-like pencils with small rubbers on their heads. I made eye contact with one of the two who had beaten me into the room.

"Morning," I offered unoffensively. I got a reply from both of them together. As if they had rehearsed it: "Morning."

Wow, that was that then. End of conversation. They were both setting up laptops and priming Dictaphones for the upcoming lecture. I didn't press them for any further communication. With my paper pad and pencils out I had done all I needed to do to prepare. So, we sat in silence for a few minutes with only the passing engines of occasional traffic disrupting the sound of their fingers striking keyboards. The only other noise was the low ticking of a cheap, red plastic clock hung on the far wall. It was the calm before the intellectual storm. Soon after, muffled voices and echoed treads that were out of step drew in. The main body of the class had arrived, about twenty or so together. I recognised a few faces from the introductory lecture and found some other faces vaguely familiar from the darkened hive of the union bar. Though I could have had drinks with all of them in the last week for all I knew. One thing I was sure of was that the vocal Reece was not amongst them. As it transpired, he had already had enough of student life and returned home. Madman! Anyway, the room that had just been so quiet erupted into hustle and bustle. I felt more comfortable with all the other people here. No need to make unsolicited chat. I appreciated the rapid shift between peace and chaos. Someone I didn't know pulled out the chair next to me and sat down. As soon as he was seated he turned toward me to introduce himself. He extended his arm with the aim to shake hands with me. I didn't want to offend, so I shook it. His vastly stronger grip squeezed my hand and he opened his mouth to speak. I took the chance to speak first.

"I'm Pete," I said. "Good morning." It felt like a social victory to have spoken first. He replied,

"Hello Pete, I'm Tim. Very pleased to meet you." His voice carried a distinctive northern tone. Well spoken, not fully Geordie but close. He wore a white, long-sleeved shirt with gold cufflinks, topped off by a shadow grey waistcoat and clear pale skin. He was clean shaven and had thick, straight, dark hair. It was slicked back to display his perfectly straight hairline. He was well built across his shoulders, undeniably handsome, and possessed the aura of someone who had money. I instantly took a dislike to him. Apart from anything else I had already memorised one person called 'Tim'. He would have to be 'Tim two'. I bet he played rugby and had a cool tattoo or two underneath that pristine shirt. Henny would no doubt have swooned over him. Doubtless all the girls would love him and that made me angry with myself because I wasn't more like him. He was the kind of person who I imagined my father would have preferred as a son. Before I could dwell further, the lecturer entered the room and he closed the door behind him.

"Good morning all. My name is Dr. Lowa, but please everyone just call me Jim." He was a man no older than forty-five and he wore a full-length dark-green overcoat that had clearly seen better days. He had ragged shoulder length black hair. It matched perfectly with his rugged, collar length black beard. He was a cross between Long John Silver and Jonathan Creek.

"Soooooo, can everyone please sign this sheet as it comes around you all. Or alternatively, don't. I ain't a fuckin' Nazi, I'm not checking anything." He spoke slowly with an Aussie twang. He looked to me as though he was on drugs. As if he had just dragged himself out of bed in time to deliver the lecture. The attendance register was passed around the desks. It started at the table farthest away from me so I'd be the last to make my mark. By the time I did, I was the twenty-third name to be put on it. I had put my official seal on Metaphysics. It was time to learn what that really meant. Dr. Lowa - 'Jim' - slumped in a chair left vacant in one of the room's corners. He shouted out,

"Sooooo, Metaphysics." A long pause followed. "Can any of you tell me what it is?"

My new best friend sat beside me answered in a confident tone without even raising his hand.

"It means 'Beyond Physics' in ancient Greek." He answered without a trace of smugness about him.

The response from Tim two was not to Dr. Lowa's liking. I took shameful enjoyment of what came next.

"No, not what it means; what it *is*. This isn't an ancient language course you know." Jim carried on, saying what he supposed Tim two was going to expand on in a mocking accent and tone.

"The title was termed by Aristotle after he had composed his works on physics in the year blah blah… After completing his works on physics, there was only one place left to explore. Beyond physics. Metaphysics etcetera etcetera."

Jim lost his mocking tone and continued.

"All of you remember that we are not here to translate, we are not here to study history. We are philosophers. We study ideas, not the historical analysis of translation." I jotted down every word and christened my notepad. Jim stood up and began to pace back and forth in front of us all. He continued with purpose,

"In this class we will be dealing with questions, deep questions. The soul, immortality, personal identity. This is the metaphysical realm and plenty of people have had a say on it. I hope you all like reading." His words were spoken with an integrity and passion I'd never heard before from an educator. It was a truly vast subject. I committed to myself that I would read, I would learn. I would know more about it than Tim two.

{Chapter 11}

|Plans|

I was a couple of months in. I was cruising. I was even popular. Each new day was better than the last. The conversations grew deeper. The work became more involved. With every sun that set I became more ingrained into the place, and the place became more ingrained in me. I had developed a strong weekly routine. I read all the background texts and supporting material. Every essay was in on time. I attended all my lectures, all my tutorials. I had become a vocal member of all my classes, unafraid to seek further clarity or to ask questions. People knew who I was. People cared about my opinion. I loved it. Every lecture was more interesting than the last. I felt as though my brain was a dry sponge and for the first time it was soaking up enlightening mineral water. I was like an athlete in training. My mind was developing and getting stronger with each new thought. It wasn't just because of reading books and writing things down. It was the ceaseless interaction with people who were going through the same process that I was. We were all simultaneously teaching and learning from one another. It was the real essence of what university education was. An unquenchable intellectual osmosis. As well as growing into my role as a diligent student, I became dedicated to the future ambition of writing some amazing thesis for life.

I had also become a real family member of the corridor. A borderline alcoholic family that drank pretty much every day. As a collective we had ventured out to the half-dozen or so of the local pubs in the town. The locals were for the most part happy to see students in their pubs. No doubt the sound of tills ringing to the lament of student loans helped that along, but it was more than that. They seemed to genuinely appreciate the fact that we didn't confine ourselves to the safety of the Students' Union. That we opened up and tried to integrate with the community. Even

Wozza, with his unfathomably strong Essex accent, had had no issues. Well, apart from when he accidently spilt a pint which belonged to the town's rugby captain the first time we were in 'The Royal Ivy'.

As the weeks rolled by, the corridor would stay up late, often till the next day, talking. We spoke about everything from politics to pornography, from the plight of the Third World to the mistakes that had been made by prominent historical figures. We spoke with such authority and unknowable arrogance. We felt as though our generation was the first to think about such things in depth. We mused that our 'information generation' would sort out all global problems when we had finished our studies and were forced back into the real world. We thought such a time was so far away in the future that it would never happen. One such conversation took place over a bottle of spiced rum and rolling tobacco at four in the morning after a hall party that had come to a premature end due to a fire alarm fault. It was a bitter Welsh morning. The wind was trying to creep through the aging joints of the kitchen's window frames. The last two left up in the kitchen were Tim and I.

"So, Pete lad. What ya gonna go off and actually do when you're finished 'ere? I mean, job market int exactly crying out for people with degrees in Philosophy." I had not given the answer any serious thought. I had plenty of time to work that part out.

"I haven't a clue really mate. Maybe I will just stay here and do some postgrad work. Maybe I will become a binman and think fascinating thoughts about what people throw away. For now, I'm just happy learning. Well, learning and drinking anyway."

Tim carried on. "Happy, aye. You think you're just going to be happy forever do ya?" The rather pessimistic tone was something we had all come to expect from Tim. I decided to shift the topic of conversation on to a much more serious and relevant question. I lit another cigarette before I asked it.

"Tim, who do you think would win in a fight between Darth Vader and M.Bison?"

"Fuck off Pete." was all I got back from him.

Several hours later, I was lying in bed, staring at the ceiling. I found myself rolling Tim's question over in my mind. Indeed, what was I going to do? I was young and drunk so I resolved to answer it when I was old and sober. I had my whole life before me and I could do anything. My only goal was to wake up the next day and enjoy what I had. To get up and feel more fulfilled than I had been the day before. Plans were distant abstract notions sailing on the horizon of my life. Sleep took me as the light of dawn crept in through the curtains.

{Chapter 12}

|End of Term One|

I couldn't believe that my first term was nearly up, but it was. In the last ten days I had taken four exams in addition to the nine essays I had also completed as per the course module requirements. Each essay had scored me at least a mark of eighty-five percent or higher. I was proud of myself. I was three months in and on course for a first. I knew that the first year counted nothing toward the actual class of degree awarded at the end of the course - that award counted only the work of years two and three - but I was proud nonetheless. I had never known how rewarding it was to work hard and see actual results from it. Seeing nothing but positive remarks scribed across my essays had a remarkably motivating effect on my psyche. I felt like there was finally something I was good at. Something I was good at and enjoyed. There was no feeling like it.

With the exams of the term finalised my thoughts passed to what came next. Three weeks back at home with Mother and Father. I didn't want to go. Granted, there had been the infrequent moment when I had missed home. The ease of maternal cooking, the free laundry service, but in truth, cooking and cleaning for yourself was not so great a chore. Thus, such thoughts passed quickly and without residual gloom. I feared that some set of circumstances would transpire to make my return after Christmas impossible. Worried I'd become ill or that the university would burn down. Totally irrational fears - but fears all the same. I worried that the freedom and joy I'd experienced over the last three months would be taken away from me. Freedoms replaced with monotony and despair. I shook myself away from such dystopian perceptions and reassured myself that in just over three weeks I'd be back in my corridor, back in my room of safe sanctuary. That thought made me feel strong enough to endure the impending break.

Alas, the hour arrived when it was time to depart north. The car was packed for what would doubtless turn out to be an excruciating drive. A lot of that packing consisted of dirty laundry. I supposed that in the grand scheme of things I was lucky. I was going home to be surrounded by family. Over the holiday period I would eat and drink to excess. I'd be given lots of nice things wrapped in shiny paper. I wouldn't have to spend a penny. I'd be warm and safe from harm and receive bountiful hugs from Mother. That was a lot more than a great deal of souls on the planet could claim. I should have been so grateful for those facts. I should have been. Maybe Henrietta would be home for the holidays too. Maybe I'd get to see her. Maybe. I started the engine, put the car into first and slowly started to move away. I had hardly used the car since arriving and I could feel the car's reluctance to move away as if it were an extension of my own. The car moved off, but not smoothly. The voyage north began to the sound of brakes creaking loose.

Christmas came and went. I was issued my standard quotient of socks, handkerchiefs and male grooming products. My 'big' present of the year had been a brand-new Oxford English Dictionary. To be fair to my parents, they hadn't long bought me a car and laptop so I kept the majority of any ungratefulness in check. Besides, I was used to such gifts, and had long since mastered the face of false gratitude.

At the main dining table, which had now seen its nineteenth Christmas dinner, I boasted righteously to my father about my consistent eighty-five percent marks for all the work I had done. He replied factually that, "Eighty-five percent isn't a hundred, is it." His reply hadn't been a question, it was a statement. I'd thought that he might have smiled a little at my achievement and said, *"Well done son."* I was wrong. Just when I thought I'd done enough to show my father that I was climbing a little in life, he knew just what to say to knock me back down into the basement of self-esteem. I couldn't fault the factual nature of his argument, but what he said, combined with his tone, made me feel slightly unwelcome at the table.

My mother's face was the polar opposite. She was delighted to have her son home. It was a strange experience, to feel simultaneously welcome and unwelcome in your family home. Maybe that was what the essence of growing up was. The kind of growing up Mr. Demptham had tried to prepare me for at Woodbourne. I had always assumed that his lectures about 'growing up' and 'becoming a man' would have come to fruition in the twenty-five to thirty age range. Perhaps I should've paid more attention to what he was actually trying to tell me rather than concerning myself about the next time Daz and I could sneak off for a smoke.

The rest of the holidays I spent on my own in my room reading. On the odd occasion, I challenged Father to a game of chess. He always won, but rather than give me any advice on tactics or strategy he contained himself to merely saying, "Concentrate," in a displeased tone after every checkmate he applied. I was a quasi-prisoner. Wishing the days away till my release back to Llantarn. I read to pass the time; to see my sentence out in peace. It wasn't like I could engage my parents in conversation regarding the finer points of Montaigne or Kant. I just read and waited. I'd received no messages or calls from the old Woodbourne bunch asking me to meet up for a drink to compare experiences. I hadn't expected to hear from anyone and didn't really care either way, apart from Henrietta. I had hoped that she might have messaged to meet and catch up. I hoped.

Henrietta: *Hey Pete, I don't suppose you're home for the holidays are you? X*

The message on my phone made my heart skip a beat or two.

Me: *Hey Henny, I sure am. XXX*

Henrietta: *That's good. Me too. Fancy meeting for a catch up? X*

Me: *Absolutely, just give me a time and a place. XXX*

Henrietta: *How about 2 o'clock tomorrow afternoon? Down the Silver Salmon? X*

I attempted to be suave in my response.

Me: *Is 3'o'clock ok? I have some stuff to do tomorrow? XXX*

Henrietta: *Sounds good to me. See you there X*

To say I was excited would have been an egregious understatement. I re-read her messages to make sure I hadn't imagined them. I had trouble sleeping that night. Maybe her first term at uni had changed her as much as mine had changed me. Maybe she was now prepared to think that there was more to a man than tattoos, big arms and six-packs. Unlikely, but possible. There was a chance, and a chance was good enough.

In spite of my falsely claiming to have had stuff to do I arrived at 'The Silver Salmon' at ten to three the following afternoon. I got a pint of IPA and a G'n'T with ice and a slice, just the way she liked it. The pub was mostly deserted and I took up position at a table in a cosy corner next to the hearth. The coal fire was glowing nicely, giving off a beautiful radiance of red light and heat. I lit up a cigarette and hypothesised about the conversation I would have with her. I dreamed she would come in, sit down, take a sip of her drink, then tell me she loved me and wanted a relationship with me. No matter the distance, we'd make it work somehow. I also imagined that she'd stood me up. I was nothing if not balanced.

It was half past three. Still no Henrietta. I had finished my pint and went to the bar for another. Sitting back down in the corner I could see the barmaid's thoughts as she looked over. *'That lad has been stood up.'* I hoped her intuition was wrong. Either way I had a delicious fresh pint. I thought about messaging her to find out where she was but decided against it as I thought it might make me seem desperate and lonely. I wasn't lonely; I had plenty of cigarettes. I lit up another. At ten to four the pub door opened and in she came. She slung her handbag over the back of the chair opposite mine and bade me to stand up. I did so and she gave me a huge hug, complete with a kiss on the cheek. The barmaid had no reason to feel smug now! We both sat. It was good to see her, yet not as good as I thought it would have been. Perhaps my time at Llantarn had served to dilute her in my mind. Somehow made her more relative. We talked and revelled, gossiped and laughed - but somehow, she seemed smaller. Less interesting. Her opinions were less important, less valid. A few short months ago, this beautiful person's perspectives would have encapsulated and invigorated me. Not now. As she continued to talk I even found myself becoming bored of her stories and new ambitions. It had transpired that the main thing I had hoped for on my homecoming was an illusion. A boy's illusion, built up in the mind. People were only important relative to their situation. That realisation was the most enlightening experience I had had thus far in life. It was also the saddest.

She left the pub a couple of hours later. She had finished her latest G'n'T, kissed me on the cheek again and departed. She was gone and I was left in the pub, next to the fire, alone. My internal state was in a form of disarray. To an outside observer, they just saw a young man quietly having an ale on his own. They couldn't know the turmoil that raised inside me. I questioned myself: *"Is this university experience actually good for me?"*

After only three months, I could easily discount a person I had once felt so deeply for. If this was what I was like after three months what would I be like after three years? Those questions rattled around me for the rest of that night, and the next night, and the next. I had to utilise my newfound reason to find a way through the pressing paradigm shift. I would use the principals of logic and deduction to resolve my woes. The tools of Philosophy should be able to help with a real-world dilemma and not just a thought experiment. If Philosophy, the subject I had chosen to devote myself to, couldn't help me with this then it wasn't worth anything. The best part of this philosophical reasoning was that it was internal; it only had to be internally consistent. It had to make coherent sense to me, but only to me. If I could use my logic and get it to make sense to me then I would be correct, regardless of what the final outcome was. So, one night about a week after my drinks with Henrietta, I drank some of my father's whiskey and stowed away in my room with nothing but some blank paper and a sharp pencil.

Question. Is the university experience good for me if I can so lightly alter long held opinions about quantities I had previously cared so deeply for?

Answer. The question must be dissected into two parts. Firstly, 'Is the university experience good for me?' and secondly, 'Is the university experience changing the way I feel about things in my life?' The answer to the first part of the question was simple. Yes. I was happy at university. I felt that I was better educated and thus in a better place to make decisions due to that fact. I was much more socially developed and would therefore become a more well-rounded and understanding member of society because of it. The higher educated senses I was developing would lead me to a level of insight that would allow me to change my mind regarding situations and scenarios as they came up. Education was the key to flexibility. Flexibility was the first step on the way to a truly open mind. A closed mind would be unable to see alternative perspectives - whether out of fear of seeming weak, or blind ignorance. A growth in knowledge and wisdom must be a positive thing if only by virtue of veering away from negative diminution.

The answer to part two of the question flowed seamlessly from the first. The growth in knowledge is required by evolutionary imperatives. We need to know more to give us the best chance of survival, whatever the next threat may be. Without growth there can be no change. Without change there can be no advancement. As we grow, things that do not grow appear smaller. In the same way, as we advance, things that do not advance seem smaller. Everything is relative. If I grow and change and others do not, then not only *should* I view them differently, but I have *no option other* than to view them differently, both physically and literally.

That was my answer. That was my philosophy in action. It became my secure truth. It made me feel better. On paper it made sense to me. It was a personal philosophical truth.

I smiled. That night I slept easy. I knew there was a multitude of other ways to interpret the question, but they didn't matter. My way was my solution, and my way was the way I would have to live with.

{Chapter 13}
|The Return of the Student|

First night back. I'd called Mother from the car as soon as I'd got parked up. It put her mind at rest to know that I had arrived back safely. With that obligatory task complete it was time to collect my bags and head inside.

A fully conscious sigh of relief was expelled when I unlocked the door to Hawson 58. I dropped my bags onto the bed and exhaled with utter tranquillity. The feeling of being home overwhelmed me. Being truly home. As I inhaled, I detected the faintest trace of stale cigarette smoke. I liked it. I opened my bags to unpack. The freedom I felt being back was so viscerally energising. I felt more alive, more awake, even after that pig of a drive. I felt like I had done on the first day of the last term, only without the pressing administrative burden of registration. Before I knew it, I had unpacked everything. My bed was made with the crisp clean sheets, lovingly laundered by Mother. The corridor was quiet. The entire building was quiet. I'd never experienced such an absence of sound from the hall before. I had returned a day early. I had not returned early due to any argumentative home life, besides the daily life lectures from my mother. I just wanted to be back. Now I was free again to talk to friends and strangers as I pleased. I opened my curtains and absorbed the view. The Welsh countryside. The Scottish countryside that I was used to seeing, the one I had grown up in, was grand. It was full of green and water-soaked vistas, but I preferred the cosy valleys of Wales. Its horizons were not as visually impressive as the ones of lower Alba, not as epic or striking - but the Welsh green had an invitational quality. It was welcoming rather than grandiose. The wind had less of a sinister bite and the sun bestowed more of a warm glow. That night, I went to the local convenience shop and got a bottle of red. Upon getting back to my room I put my laptop's music media player onto random and waited for sleep to come for me with innocent purple lips. I drifted off to the sound of charts gone by, the philosophers of sound. That night, I slept with the curtains open.

I woke with a stretch. I knocked over the empty bottle of red wine. I yawned with youthful liberation and reached for my lighter. I saw my phone. Its digital readout read, '26 New Text Messages'. My waking malaise instantly transformed into panic. My mind raced, it jumped to conclusions. My initial thought was, *"Someone has died."* This was followed shortly by, *"Someone has died, must be family. Must be immediate family."* My heart rate elevated rapidly. I felt a hot surge of adrenaline; I shook a little. I calmed down, I remembered. Due to the lack of proper network coverage in Llantarn, messages took an age to load. The messages loaded, at last.

You have message(s) from: Ste- Wozza- Tim- Dill- Flitzy- Neil- Paul- Danny

My pulse slowed. Nothing from my family; that must be a good and non-urgent sign. As I examined the content of the messages that I had been sent, I started to grin, then fully smile, then laugh. They all read along the same lines of "We gettin' smashed tonight?" Relieved, I closed my clamshell phone and lit up my morning cigarette. I looked outside my window and was greeted by the soft grey shine of a January morning. The sun was bright but its messengers were cold. The dew on the ground outside lay heavy but it shimmered and sparkled as though the green grass was laden with tiny diamonds. The beauty of that image helped me to breath and equalise myself. I'd had a nasty shock, a worrisome personal incident. I was relieved that none of my family were dead or seriously ill. I planned to call home and tell them how much I loved them. I planned to. I didn't.

{Chapter 14}
|The Second Term|

It wasn't term two, it was term squared! It had started out much in the same vein as term one had concluded. The glorious academic rhythm of lectures, tutorials and essay deadlines had returned. As had the alcohol fuelled corridor debates. In the fifth week of the term I handed in an essay on the speculative unity of the respective philosophies of Heraclitus and Parmenides. Academically, I was firing on all cylinders. Socially too I continued my advance into popular desirability, though not to the same extent as the rugby players. My social encounters expanded with every week that passed. Invitations to parties and events were constant, and people genuinely cared if I attended or not. At points, I even became aware of people being sycophantic toward me. Aside from feelings of consternation about it, I was flattered. How had it happened? Peter Morgan had become someone to be seen to be friends with. Both on the academic circuit and social scene I had become worthy in the eyes of my peers. I understood why it was the case in the academic domain as I spent a lot of time in the library reading and researching my subject, but socially? I had just been myself, and that was apparently enough.

I found the most extraordinary part of the whole experience was that it was organic in genesis. I hadn't set out an agenda. There was no planned strategy on how to become well-liked or respected. Just by expressing myself honestly, it evolved. As far as I could tell I had been just the same at school, apart from the academic integrity, but at Woodbourne my character had apparently demoted my social stance. At Llantarn my character served to enhance my status. The rise in morale that resulted from it no doubt aided my academic output. My studies had progressed so prodigiously that I started to ponder serious thoughts about doing postgraduate work. Lofty notions indeed for a first-year student in his second term.

I still maintained the weekly check-in chat with home which served as a good opportunity for the universe to suck some of my positivity away. At the commencement of every call I started out as an educated and empowered professional student, by the time I'd hung up the phone I was a naughty primary school boy. As soon as the conversation ended, the positives rushed back into me. I could take the thirty minutes of negativity to be happy for the rest of the week. Weeks filled to the brim with smiles, laughs and booze.

Despite my new found popularity, I never put any new social circle or person ahead of the corridor troop, the good old 'Whore Sons'. We all felt that we had bonded like a platoon in a war film, only we would surely never have to face 'The Big Push'. We'd spent so much time together, often drunk, that we knew each other inside out. In the darkest hours of the night we'd bare the fantasies of our souls for all to hear. Memories and musings that none amongst us would have dared share with any others. Such projections were always met with grace and good humour, displaying the best symptoms of the human condition. Dave spoke about his memories of seeing his dad hit his mum. Wozza spoke of his impossible yearning to speak to his deceased step-dad. Ste spoke about his fiancée killing herself from an accidental heroin overdose. All I could expose about myself were the unrequited feelings I had had for Henrietta, and how sad I was that I no longer had them. I had nothing on the same level as the other guys, no sorrow nor hardship, but it wasn't a competition. Nobody looked for sympathy. Perhaps we all just wanted an avenue of escape or a shoulder to shed a drunken tear, but never pity. No, pity was never sought or unduly given. We all offered each other open minds and open ears. It couldn't have been any more different to the life I'd had at home.

There was one night in February, we were all sat in Wozza's room, watching an old episode of 'Sharpe' on DVD. The whole corridor was crammed in there. Three on the bed, one in the chair and the rest making do on the floor. We had all had a few beers and were relentlessly, lovingly insulting each other. I just sat back and had a crystalline perception: *"This is my real family."* It certainly felt like it at the time.

Yet, the more I thought about it the more it troubled me. I was an aspiring philosopher. I hoped that I would one day produce a work of significance, a thesis. That sometime in the future a group of students would analyse and interpret my work. I was not conceited enough to have thought that I would write anything of the importance like the 'Tractatus' or 'Beyond Good and Evil', but I wanted to at least manufacture something that would add a brick to the wall of human comprehension. Philosophy was like a set of building blocks. If you wanted to construct a strong and stable matrix then you needed strong and stable foundations upon which to build. Such solid substratum must originate in the mind of the designer. To understand philosophy required you to become a scientist of ideas. If you wanted to be able to create a work of your own, then you needed to be a robust mental architectural engineer as well. Whether it was metaphysics, epistemology or ethics, the progression of logic and reason were paramount. That is what bothered me so much.

When I had got back to my room after Christmas and had forgotten about the crappy mobile phone network coverage issue, I had seen that I had twenty-six new message notifications. At that point my mind made irrational leaps to death and despair. Negative leaps. In those few seconds of internal turmoil there was no logic, no calm reasoning process, just conclusions with no justifications. I mulled over the issue for several weeks without resolution. The more I examined it the worse I felt. There I was, a would-be professional philosopher, irrational and illogical. I tried using my process of philosophical deduction to find some sort of conclusion, the way I had done with Henrietta at Christmas. It only resulted in dead ends, wasted paper and cigarette butts. I was frustrated and irritated with myself. I felt like I was philosophically fucked. The situation would have been ideal if I were an aspiring poet.

{Chapter 15}

|'B'|

It was mid-March. The days were growing slightly longer and marginally warmer. I had reached a resolution of sorts regarding my personal doubts about my future ability to write something of worth. I had settled my worries with the idea that the calm and totally rational mind took time to develop. Through the further study of my subject and added life experience from living, I would develop into a mind that would be able to produce something of value. It wasn't a solid basis for feeling better about the situation; it was too hopeful. But that's what I had to work with going forward, so that's what I would hang on to for the time being.

I was in 'The Royal Ivy', one of the pubs in town, alone. I loved drinking in the union bar and the corridor kitchen but after so many weeks it had started to get a tad repetitive. I hadn't classed its repetitive nature as a negative thing, but a change was as good as a rest. Each of the pubs in town had its own peculiarities, as did any pub in the land. These could not be readily absorbed when going into them for a quick beer on a pub crawl. Each public house has a certain charm that is unique. It took time to comprehensively appreciate what those charms were. Every carpet stain and faded painting held a story - the amalgamation of all of those shadowed tales created a pub's character. You needed to take the time to let that character soak in. Some pubs specialised in darts, some in pool. Others would have champion dominoes players whilst others focussed on playing cards. But all of them were unique. So, I drank in all of them equally.

Every so often I would just slink off from the Hawson pack and have a little alone time. We all did it to some degree. Humans, we all need a bit of alone time now and then. That day, I was enjoying mine. It meant I would be missing out on a Stella-fuelled vampire movie marathon in Ste's room, but I was willing to take that hit. With my first

pint I contemplated the latest philosophical dilemma
which had been presented in one of the week's lectures.
By the end of that pint I was fairly sure I had developed a
pretty sound counter argument to the proposition. I sat
alone, I felt altogether rather pleased with myself.

'The Royal Ivy' had two separate entry/exit points at
opposite ends of the building. The pub was split in two by
a partition wall but had only the one bar that served both
sides. I was sat in the primary lounge bar, the one you
walked into straight from the High Street. The secondary
room behind the wall had the pool table and the toilets.
Whenever I was in one of the pubs in town I used to
broaden my soft Scottish accent a bit. I'd even throw in
some regional wordage such as 'ken', 'wee' and 'dram'.
Somehow, I felt that I'd be more well received if I
sounded more national to the native residents of the town.
They may well be happy to have students spend their
money in their shops and pubs but they were still Welsh
after all! I'd used the facilities after I'd finished my first
pint and hadn't seen a soul in the pool room. After I sat
back down with my second pint the two other people I'd
been sharing the main room with left. It was just me. Just
me, alone, with fresh beer: the peace I had craved was
upon me. I brought out the small copy of 'The Tao Te
Ching' I had in my pocket and began reading as I drank.

> *'Allow the heart to empty itself*
> *of all turmoil!*
> *Retrieve the utter tranquillity of mind*
> *from which you issued.'*

Drinking and thinking in peace was certainly the way to
try and absorb it. Pint two turned into pint three, four, five
and six, with an additional spiced rum.

After reaching my limit with Lao Tze, I put my book away
and took stock. The main bar now had at least a dozen
people in it. I didn't recall any of them coming in, but I
had been focussed on reading some deep and interesting
stuff. It was half past nine already. *"Wow,"* I thought,
"Time flies when you read Tao." My bladder acutely
informed me of its need to evacuate its contents before

pint seven could be indulged. I went through the pool room to the familiar gents' door, but before I made it there, my life changed.

Our eyes met. I discovered a new state of being. A stillness I'd thought exclusive to Buddhist monks. She was perfect in ways I could never hope to qualify with words or quantify with numbers. Time became irrelevant. The universe froze around her. She could re-write the laws of physics if she willed it. I thought she could see my heart beating out of my chest, the adrenaline forcing it out of my ribs onto a plate for her. She could make it dance like a puppet at her behest. Traumatic and divine harmonics shook me from socks to soul. Light and life had new meanings defined. I had never conceived of anything in all of existence that would make it possible. There was *no* logic, *no* rational explanation for the experience. She looked at me up and down quizzically.

"Can I get you a drink?" came like distant silk from her lips.

"Yes please," came the polite voice of a primary school boy. One who had forgotten he even had a bladder to empty. My mind was ablaze. *"What is happening to me? Am I having a stroke of some kind?"* I reassured myself in the negative. I had no trouble walking to the bar with her and could at least speak to confirm I wanted a drink. At the bar she asked,

"So, what would you like?"

I didn't know. So I just blurted a, "Yes." I was lost in the mercurial landscape of her hazel eyes. I knew then and there I'd do anything for her, give her anything she asked, tell her anything she wanted to know. There is neither academy nor algorithm to prepare you for love at first sight. I thought about all the cynics in the world who would never believe in such a thing; they had nothing but my deepest sympathies.

We drank that night away together. Every minute that passed ensnared me deeper into her web. When we kissed, I was like a man who'd seen dawn for the first time. That moment etched into my soul for all time. The feeling was so inflammatory and luminous. It was the source of all poetry. It was what had sent a thousand ships to war and what had truly shattered the hearts of the Romantics. We kissed again; she wrapped her fingers around the base of my skull as if trying to rip off my head in arachnoid fashion. I understood why the male of the species allowed them to. I was so lost, so utterly powerless. My life would never be the same. Her name was Belladonna-Elizabeth, but she preferred to just be called, 'B'.

{Chapter 16}

|Dawn Truth|

I woke up. I was in my bed in Hawson. It must have been a dream. Experiences like that only happen in dreams. I was barely semi-conscious and reached for my pack of smokes. After I'd shaken three empty packs I heard the comforting dull rattle of a half-full packet. I had a bad head, that much was unmistakable. I needed water desperately, though a smoke took top priority. Whilst smoking I tried to move my head as little as possible. I glanced at the time: 11:56. *"Oh well, that's lectures missed for today then."*

My room baked in the dull glow of the sun as its rays penetrated through the meek curtains. It gave my room a friendly reddish hue, a new atmosphere to my sanctuary I had not yet experienced as the spring, my first Llantarn spring, was in its initial ascendance. It was pushing back the winter to bring its resurgent green to the fore. I drew in on my cigarette and inhaled very, very deeply with closed eyes in an attempt to stitch together the veiled and fractured pieces of the previous night. I tapped my ash away and wondered, *"Was she a dream?"* I bravely rotated my head around as I tried to shake away the haze of the booze enciphered headache. I felt an unusual pain. I stubbed out my cigarette and felt towards the back of my neck with curious fingers. It felt like a welt, like a pronounced scratch.

In one bound I was in front of the mirror. I investigated with hope. I could just about see it. It looked like it had been caused by a fingernail. I flashed back to that first kiss, to all the kisses that came after it, her hands that cupped my skull; she gripped me, she broke the skin. She wasn't a dream, she was real - I knew her name. I announced it aloud to myself in the mirror. "B." The actualities of the previous night flooded back to me like an overwhelming tsunami of emotion. I was in love. I scrambled for my phone and in the process I gave myself the worst toe stubbing in all of human history. I expelled the loudest, "AAAAAAHHHHHHHHHHHHH BASTARD" that Hawson Hall must have ever heard. I collapsed onto my bed and clutched my throbbing foot in one hand whilst the other reached out for my phone. I grabbed it and flipped it open. The network logo was displayed showing that I did actually have some coverage at the time, however, that was all it displayed. There were no new messages and no missed calls. I opened my contacts menu to check for any newly added contacts listed under 'B'. There were none. I frantically checked all the contact numbers in my phone for anything new or out of the ordinary, again there was nothing.

I closed my phone and sat dejected. The pulsating physical pain in my toe became somehow trivial. I lit up another cigarette and thought to myself, *"At least she is real."* The tenderness in my freshly swelling toe did enough to ensure that I wasn't dreaming. She wasn't a dream, wasn't a mere figment of youthful, lustful imagination. I had to find her as soon as possible. I would talk to everyone I knew; I would use every resource I could to find her. I was in love: it was my duty to knock on every door on campus to find her, and I'd knock them down if I had to! If I didn't find her by doing that then I'd knock down every door of every student house in town too! My life had developed new priorities. New focus. Find B, whatever the cost, whatever the effort, however long it would take. I had never known such resolve.

There was a knock at my door. I hobbled over to answer it.

It was B.

{Chapter 17}
|The Summer of '06|

1st May

B and I spent every second of every day together. I had
never known or imagined a bond between two people as
that which we felt. Each time I saw her I fell in love again,
deeper. An intense exponential symphony of feeling. I had
hardly seen the guys from the corridor since meeting her:
it didn't matter, I didn't care. I hardly went to a seminar or
attended a lecture. Again, I didn't care. All those flattering
new feelings of popularity and respect faded into
irrelevance. Suffice to say that the only thing that did
actually matter was being with her. She opened my eyes to
new ways of thinking, her intellect and character were so
utterly unique. We'd lie naked together for hours, days
even. She'd read Ginsberg with an old Bill Hicks show
playing in the background; we'd both smoke. I'd light one
up and watch the tendrils of smoke dance across her bare
flesh, watch the trail follow her spine down to her waist
and funnel over her hips. I'd reach out a hand and place it
firmly on her back just to remind myself that I could.
She'd twist her neck and look at me with pure and total
love. She'd kiss me with her eyes as well as her lips.
Those eyes, the deepest hazelnut eyes I had ever seen.
Eyes that gave the impression that she knew something
that nobody else in the world did.

After weeks of living that way we decided we should
actually go for a night in the union bar with our combined
friend groups. We were supposed to meet down there at
seven, but the blasting sun beaming down during the day
was too good to waste. We collectively decided to have a
day session by the river instead. It was a glorious twenty-
six degrees and there wasn't a breath of wind. B and I
arose at eleven, which was comparatively early for us. I
left her room in Ivan Simones Hall to round up the

Hawson gang so we could head into town for supplies and pick up one of those disposable barbeques.

An hour or so later, we all descended on the riverbank. Pretty much every other group on campus had had the same idea and the riverbanks were swarming with dozens of university community gatherings. The rugby players passed a ball back and forth; the martial arts lot were trying to throw one another over on the grass; the footballers kicked a ball about between themselves - the scenes went on. It was like a scene from an American teen movie. The Hawson cohort I was part of crossed the short footbridge which joined one side of the campus to the other and as we did, I easily made out the sight of B and her friends sat right down the bottom end of the bank where the waterflow entered the campus boundary. She stood and waved at us just to be sure we had seen them. We ventured over and seated ourselves on the soft warm grass in a close hollow square. Seeing as it was Llantarn most of the people in our respective friend groups had met each other at one time or another so there was no lengthy introductions process required. I placed myself right down next to B onto a red tartan picnic blanket she had brought out from somewhere. As I settled down she leaned into me. It felt so natural, so right. Ste set up his portable speaker and played some chilled-out acoustic tunes as everyone cracked open a beer and began to relish in the day.

At the request of several like-minded music fans in the new super-group I popped back to my room to grab a couple of my Pink Floyd CDs that I'd looted from my father. On my way back I just had to stop. I was about halfway back over the footbridge and I halted to take stock and just look. I stood there, CDs in hand, leant over the rusted rail. I just stared at her. I couldn't do anything else. I could have spent the rest of my life inside that one point in time. Such a perfect, beautiful moment. It was as though she was the only person who existed out of all the people sat there. I carried on walking yet that singular feeling persisted. She was the only truth in my world, and I was walking towards her. I sat back next to her, kissed her, and we laid down together to feel the open warmth of the Welsh sun massage our faces. We sat back up together when the joint came our way: we'd puff away a few times and inhale/exhale into each other's lungs with lips pressed tightly closed before laying back down. Though the music played, our ears heard only the sound of laughter and cool running water with the occasional birdsong. She whispered in my ear.

"I love you."

I gave her then most simple and honest reply I could have.

"I love you too." I thought that life could never possibly get any better. I was right.

1st June

As I opened my eyes the light hit them. It hurt them. The stench of stale weed hung heavy in the warm close air of her room. I shifted my head slightly to get a view of the time displayed on her laptop. I had done it again. My Early Greek Philosophy exam had started five hours ago – hell, it had finished two hours ago. It had been the final exam of my first year; in total there had been six end-of-year exams to academically complete the year. I had only managed to make it to one of them, and I had virtually no recollection of what I'd written in it. I had even less recall of the questions themselves - I didn't even remember which module the exam was for! That was probably due to the fact that I was thoroughly stoned for its entirety.

For the last four, maybe five weeks, B and I had done remarkably little other than get high and fuck. Both of us had allowed our academic obligations to fall away till there was nothing but skin and skins. With every inhalation and every orgasm we died a little inside each other, both drawn further away from that sunshine peak by the river.

I popped back to my room in Hawson to get a Dire Straits CD I wanted us to listen to. All I could think about was getting back to her. I needed to get back to her, back to her smell. Get back to her eyes, either awake and loving or asleep and dreaming. I loved just watching her when she slept, though my soul lusted for her to wake and remind me that I wasn't alone in the world. The thought that one day we'd be separated terrified me; it made me hold her more tightly every day. When I returned she stirred and awoke. She looked at me in the dim light of her room. Seduction and fatigue unified into one mesmerising glance.

"What time is it?" she asked in her dull semi-lucid tone.

"It's gone four," I answered as softly as I could.

"Did you miss your exam?" she enquired placidly.

"Yeah, but it doesn't matter."

"It doesn't?"

"No," I stressed as reassuringly as I could. "Nothing matters apart from us." I whispered as I placed my hand squarely upon her chest between her breasts. Her dark eyes closed as my palm made contact with her. Her breathing deepened and she sat up on the bed. She brought both of her hands to rest atop of mine. She reopened her eyes displaying a dark lusty stupor, luscious like new treacle. She swung her hips and manoeuvred her legs round so she was sat on top of me. Her tight frame pulled and manipulated me into collapsing on top of her, face to face. She blinked, she kissed me.

The next four weeks passed in a further psychedelic sexual haze that my memory would never be able to penetrate. All I could recollect were flashes, some specific incidents, but nothing in terms of context or temporal order. Other than particular events, I had fuzzy memories of B and I smoking down by the river. That is where we met the 'Circle'.

1st July

I had been smoking weed every day for about eight weeks straight so I had built up a slight level of tolerance for it. My brain must have adapted its ability to create or search for memories as I could remember more day to day activities. B and me would go down to the riverbank, bathe in the sun and smoke weed whenever we could. One afternoon, whilst we were walking to our normal location, she recognised a few people from her English Literature course sat by the river. She decided we should say 'hello' and so we sat with them. As soon as we did, we became aware of a couple of joints working their way around the group. Clearly this was a group of free thinkers sustaining supremely deep conversations...

"The Phantom Menace wasn't that bad!"

"Picard was much better than Sisko!"

"The Matrix sequels were actually awesome!"

"Slash was actually way more culturally significant than Axel!"

"Obviously, Alien would beat Predator in a fair fight!"

Lines such as those were thrown around the group like verbal ping-pong balls. They were all nice and friendly people; friendly passionate people. Each one tried frenetically to argue their irrelevant point whilst attempting to listen to the other points being kicked about at the same time. All the while at least two of them were skinning up. The arguments carried on till the presenter had something to smoke offered to their lips, then afterwards they'd carry on as if unbroken. B was passed a joint much fatter than one we would ever smoke, she took it in deep several times, then she looked at me and smiled. After inhaling it for myself I had a moment of existential introspection. I thought, if someone a year ago had told me, *"Oh yeah Pete, this time next year you'll just walk over to a group of people you don't know, sit down with them and smoke drugs with them all"* I would have been horrified. I'd have seen myself as some sort of immoral dope fiend from an Irvine Welsh novel.

Yet, that is essentially what had happened that day. Nobody died or got robbed, it was just a natural experience for all. It wasn't desperation, it was just, nice. It was the kind of nice that reminded me of that cup of tea I had had in my first week in the non-smoking café in town. It was, again, simply rather lovely.

There were seven of them in their self-styled 'Circle'. Jayne, an overtly hippy woman approaching her middle fifties who had a great deal of warmth and maternity to complement her outstanding music knowledge. She spent a good deal of time talking to B about the particular healing energies of certain crystals. She had the hint of a West Country accent and was more than a touch overweight, but it was hard to properly assess as we were all sat down on the grass.

One space to the left of Jayne was a rather plump, exceedingly Welsh girl with very short black hair which included a red streak. She was called Rachel. Her tattoos of Welsh dragons emblazoned on both ankles were overtly striking. She hadn't seemed to even notice that B and I had sat down. At the time she had been speaking very energetically about all of David Tennant's faults in his portrayal of Doctor Who to the young woman immediately to her left, whilst she simultaneously rolled another spliff.

The girl on the receiving end of the tirade was called Jackie and appeared athletic and toned in frame. She was also robust in voice. A well-spoken voice of discernible diction. I liked her.

"For fuck sake Rachel, are you going to stop speaking long enough to finish rolling that?" she spat with volume and vector. Initially I thought it was a strong statement of annoyance but I later found out that the heightened exclamation was some sort of private joke between them. Rachel finished rolling and sparked it up. After a couple of puffs, she passed it to Jackie.

"Finally," Jackie snapped with a fake hyper-cynicism. She took the spliff and began to wheeze away at it. She had an angular face. She wasn't ugly, far from it. She was pronounced, almost regal in a way, despite the fact that her dress sense had been lifted directly from the nineteen seventies. Her skin was a fusion of silk with coconut and her long dark brown hair flowed free. When she noticed B and me, after she'd passed the joint on, she extended her right hand for us both to shake. B and I indulged the oddly formal greeting; we had no reason not to.

"I'm Jackie, pleased to make your acquaintances." That was that from her, for now.

Next again to Jackie was Judy. She was Canadian, obviously unbeknownst to me at the time. She was verbose and to my ears sounded American. She took humoured offence at my attempt to start an introductory conversation with her.

"So, what part of America are you from then?" I asked in innocence. I was met with a stern glance and dead pan answer.

"The Canadian part."

I dried my teeth and apologised for any national offence I may have inadvertently caused. She smiled graciously and hesitantly testified, "Apology accepted." She still sounded American to me though.

The three remaining persons were all male. Adrian, Lyle and Kof. Adrian was the most softly spoken of the three, with a weak accent-less voice that coupled neatly with his child's body. Despite only being nineteen he was completely bald. Lyle was most unusual to look at. Lyle was missing several teeth from his front row and wore the most psychedelic knitted hoodie ever made. He was supremely proud of the fact that it was handmade in Nepal - the fact he himself had never been to Nepal, or even out of Wales didn't seem to matter to him. He had thin and greasy shoulder length hair but was tremendously friendly and laughed more than any of the rest. That just left Kof. Kof was a gentle giant. He had spikey black yet receding hair. He wore small glasses on the end of his nose. I always thought he resembled the old badger from 'The Animals of Farthing Wood' - though his intellect and social skills were blatantly extremely underdeveloped.

None of the group were in the slightest bit threatening and they definitely had an ample supply of particularly good green stuff. I relaxed and smoked it. My quick five-minute analysis of the group had in fact taken me five hours. What an open group of people. The Hawson boys were great, but they liked to maintain a sense of bravado in some aspects. I still liked them all, but this 'Circle' was something else entirely.

{Chapter 18}

|Round and Round|

When you are in a communal group whose friendship is fundamentally based on the fact that you all take drugs then you're not in a comradely team, you are in a narcotic collective farm. You form part of a co-operative, just a member of an alliance of convenience. The chemicals released in the body whilst in the company of the group deliver a powerfully warm and secure place to stay. A place to hide. A cosy cocoon of invulnerability which is more intoxicating than any ale or spirit produced by legal means. You want those feelings to be real so much that you make yourself believe that they are. As does everyone else around you. Everyone indulges in a false ultra-security, and all feel better for it because the illusion is a shared one. The illusion that it is actually real. The dream that it would last forever. Fantasy, reality, it didn't matter to me. Whether it was real or not, I had B, and *that* was all that mattered. I had B.

B and I spent the scant remaining weeks of the summer term with the 'Circle'. B had been more willing than I to experiment with different substances. I had only sampled my first taste of weed after I'd met B. Since I'd arrived in Llantarn, I had drunk a lot - a hell of a lot; I had smoked countless cigarettes; and after meeting B I had done quite a lot of weed. I undeniably enjoyed smoking that stuff. The hazy massage of scalp and spine was topped only by its ability to unlock long forgotten doorways in the mind. Eclectic memories of childhood interweaved with notions about the true nature of life and the universe. The speed of light aside the speed of my first push bike. Was it that 'Third Eye' I had read about now being open to see? I could see connections and feel parallels and patterns where before I saw only grey. Even staring at the ceiling transformed my creative mind into a dream factory of self-indulgent cake and gold. Completely unable to scribe any of those insights onto paper for fear that if I tried, I would lose my train of thought and stray from further enlightenment. That herb repeatedly took me to the edge of cognitive innocence and sin. I would have been content to get off the drug-train at that stop. I was unsure how to feel about trying anything else. B though was always game for a new experience. She never placed any pressure on me to do stuff with her, but I'd be damned if I was going to miss out on any possible experience that could bring us even closer together.

Within the social perimeter of the 'Circle', B and I did shrooms, coke, speed, MDMA and various other pills and prescriptions. I hadn't heard of a lot of it, but if she did it then I did it with her. Some of it was good, some of it was not. B and I both agreed to draw the line at heroin. Not that that was the kind of thing the members of the 'Circle' were into, but it felt good to have some sort of shared boundary. Whatever we took, with each other or with other 'Circle' members, nothing really bad ever happened.

By the end of those final few weeks of summer term, mine and B's excitement for the group began to wane. Every day had followed a similar pattern, and as the end of year date loomed large, we longed for more days in bed, isolated, just the two of us.

The days would go something like this:

15:00: Wake up beside B. Stare at her in wonder. Watch her wake. Fuck. Smoke a joint. Fuck again.

16:00: Eat something. Normally a large vat of toast and margarine spread.

17:00: Go out on an expedition to one of the 'Circle' houses or hall rooms.

18:00: Settle in, in whatever venue we had reached. Smoke weed, play video games, watch movies, smoke weed, engage in pointless discussion about the inaccuracies of 'Back to the Future' or something similar. Being stoned severely limited one's ability to coherently follow an argument, or properly construct one.

During the repetitive evenings of video games and pointless discussions there would always be a film playing away in the background somewhere. The same titles rotated endlessly round, 'Fear and Loathing in Las Vegas', 'Withnail and I', 'Saving Grace', 'Trainspotting', 'Twin Town', 'Requiem for a Dream', 'Spun', 'Where the Buffalo Roam', 'Human Traffic', 'The Wall' and 'The Business'. We would take drugs whilst watching films about people taking drugs. The constant repetition started to grate a little. But every night I'd look over and see B. She'd be sat there with a glazed smile and she'd look right back at me and I'd remember that nothing mattered as long as I had her.

06:00: Return to B's room, smoke weed, fuck, sleep.

With the end of term only two weeks away I was severely worried. Every day that passed put another brick in my chest. B and I had a rapidly diminishing amount of time together before reality would claim us. To make matters significantly worse, she had developed a cold.

"I love you Pete, but just go back to your room for a while," she managed to get out through her mucus-ridden nose and inflamed throat. "Pete, I will share anything with you, but I don't think we need to share these germs. Go down the bar and have a drink with all those people you've been discarding because of me. You haven't seen them properly in ages. I will be fine, I don't need looking after." Despite not wanting to be parted from her for a second, she did have a valid point. I didn't want a cold. Who the hell actually wants a cold anyway! It had been some time since I had shown my 'popular' face down in the union bar. I was surely overdue an appearance. It felt like a long time ago, the bar, the parties, the 'Whore Sons'. A long time ago.

As I left her hall and walked into the soft afternoon sunshine, the bite of the Welsh winter seemed like a lifetime ago. I strolled back to my room in Hawson and tried to figure out the last occasion that I had actually spent time with any of the corridor crowd. I honestly couldn't remember, probably that perfect day by the river with the baking sunlight and birdsong, probably… My brain felt slow, soft and pliable. I was mentally sluggish and bereft of crisp, clinical thinking. Somehow the multi-task of walking and thinking had become an extreme demand. I put it down to general fatigue, lack of vitamins and likely low blood sugar. I walked into my corridor, the corridor that had once held such safety and promise now brought slight anxiety and nerves. There was sound. Sound coming from the kitchen. Those early days blessed me with the fierce enquiry to go in and get involved, to become part of whatever was going on. I hesitantly pushed the door open and entered. The noise ceased. Sat inside were Ste, Dave, Dill, Wozza, Danny and Tim. They were surrounded by half empty wine bottles and also accompanied by a couple of rather attractive young women who I'd never met before. They all seemed somewhat disappointed to see me. Ste broke the silence.

"Alright?" he stated in a matter-of-fact voice. I decided to reply with a bit of positivity and enthusiasm.

"Yeah, really good mate, really good, cheers." My reply was met with nought but awkward silence. A silence that I decided to break.

"It's really good to see you all. Sorry I haven't been around much." That was met by a couple of rumbled nods and a thumbs up from Wozza. I realised I was not an overly welcome addition to the kitchen at that time so made an excuse to leave them all to it.

"Well, have a good night." I offered with a masked jovial tone. I was met with a muffled crossed-unison of "Will do" and "You too."

I let the kitchen door close and audibly put the key into my room lock, turned it, opened, then let the door swing clearly closed. I had in fact stayed where I was in the corridor outside the kitchen door, now with an ear pressed up smartly against the timber. A female voice asked forthrightly, "Who was that?"

To which came the response in Ste's finest Scottish timbre, "Ah that's Pete. He was sound for a while but he go' in wi that hippy druggie crowd and he stopped botherin' wi all of us."

"Oh right," she noted. That was that. They didn't spend another syllable discussing me. The next utterance was about some band or other and some soundless opinion about their music.

I decided to retire to my room for real at that point. I silently opened and closed my door. I sat on my bed and lit up a cigarette. It was the first unhappy cigarette I could remember smoking in Llantarn. I wanted the comfort of being with B so badly but knew I couldn't have it, so instead I opened up my phone and looked for an avenue to a narcotic solution. I soon found one of those.

"Great, I'll be round in ten" I affirmed before I snapped my phone shut.

{Chapter 19}

|Foolish Actions of a Young Man|

On my way to Jackie's house I contemplated, with
difficulty, what I had done with my first year at university.
To progress to the second year of the course all that had
been required of me was to get a forty percent average
throughout the year. Due to my academic inactivity of late
there was no chance that I had hit that meagre academic
bar. That train of thoughts led me to the worrying
consequences of what would come to pass in the real
world. I had become a comfortable resident of the Llantarn
'Bubble' to the point that it was the real world that now
felt abstract. Abstract, yet inescapable. I was in a mindset
of mental discord and the thought of getting to Jackie's to
have a good smoke with the rest of the 'Circle' was the
only thing I could cling to as a certainty at the time. The
community atmosphere would make me feel better, as
would any of the drugs kicking about within it. My pace
quickened.

'KNOCK KNOCK!' went the knocker. I heard light
footsteps approach. As the door opened it was Jackie stood
there. She smiled, showing her perfect teeth.

"Hey man, come on in" she requested, in a most
welcoming demeanour.

I had never been inside Jackie's place before. She was a
second year and had a little place in town. B and I had met
her at her front door a couple of times previously, before
we'd headed off to some other location. I followed inside a
step and a half behind her. Her long dark hair flowed
around the 'Dark Side of the Moon' album cover t-shirt
that she wore. A t-shirt that was perfectly form fitted. It
caressed her firm shape as though it had been sprayed on.
We entered her lounge which contained a futon with
several faux fur covers. Next to the futon was a small table
which held an ashtray, a smouldering joint and a small
ornate wooden box. There were also a couple of purple

and red arm chairs, along with a TV and associated music system with multicoloured drapes sprawled absolutely everywhere.

"I love the top," was the first thing I could think to say. It was a true statement.

"Thank you," she said as she sat herself down with poise.

There was an incredibly potent smell of weed; it was a highly encouraging sign. The walls were a similar dirty cream as the walls in Hawson but were patched over with cheap posters as well as the drapes. Led Zeppelin, King Crimson, Jimi Hendrix, Black Sabbath, Rainbow, Iron Maiden, Deep Purple, Pink Floyd. I'd never realised she had such good musical taste. The Pink Floyd poster she had up was one of six girls sat naked on the side of a swimming pool, with six different Pink Floyd album covers painted on their backs: the 'Back Catalogue'. I loved that poster.

She took the glowing joint from the ashtray, held it in her fingers and sucked wantonly. I removed my jacket and slung it over one of the armchairs. I started to sit myself down on the same chair.

"No! Don't sit all the way over there," she directed as she twiddled the spliff in her fingers showing her dexterity and her multicoloured fingernails. Her movement suggested that the effort of sharing it across an entire room would be too great. I stood immediately and took up a seated position next to her on the futon. I had never spent any time alone with Jackie before. We had always been happy associate members of the 'Circle'. The situation was a great opportunity to talk to her and get to know her better before the rest of them turned up. A more intimate chance to speak without all of the repetitive irrelevant sci-fi chat that was so prevalent in our group. As my body settled, I asked,

"When is everyone else getting here then?" assuming that the normal 'Circle' contributors would be attending as well.

"Others?" she responded quizzically. She expanded. "Everyone else has come down with a rather torrid cold by all accounts."

I remarked, "B has got it too."

"I guess we must be immune," she claimed as she tapped the ash into the tray and passed it over to me.

"Guess so," I replied taking the spliff from her taut fingers. There was only a puff or two left in it. I inhaled them both and felt the hot searing stream of the drug filter into my lungs. I stubbed it out and she stood up. She moved towards the set of audio speakers and pulled out a stack of CDs.

"I'm guessing that Pink Floyd is OK with you?" she asked in a semi-rhetorical manner.

"The Floyd is always good with me. Which albums do you have?" I responded, hoping to exploit an opportunity to flex my Pink Floyd knowledge.

"All of them, of course," she boasted enticingly.

"Well, in that case, I'm in the mood for a bit of The Division Bell."

"Good choice," she said as she rifled through a handful of discs. She found it and slipped it into the player. The smooth atmospheric sounds started to envelop the smoky room. She sat back down and stared at me. She shuffled a little closer. I spoke,

"I love this album; I mean it's by no means their most significant work, but I feel like I can close my eyes and have the sounds gently nurse my mind. It's not as brash as 'The Wall', or as ground-breaking as 'Dark Side', nor as personal as 'Wish', but it has something none of the other records do. It has a maturity, a reservation. It's like listening to a green vale. A sad green vale. In every track you get the sense that it is the end of something. Sure, they might go on and make more records together or produce more solo work. But this is the sound of nostalgia and pain neatly wrapped in a veneer of aged regret." I stopped talking, realising the amount of shite that I had just spewed from my lips. I had talked myself to distraction and hadn't even noticed Jackie reach for her box. She had opened it and started to roll up another, just for the two of us. The silken vectors of guitar and piano danced gracefully around the room and around again. She broke the ambiance.

"So, what you're saying is, that this album, this amalgamation of sad and melancholy songs is an audio message to us all about making the most out of youth and seizing the day. Because once the sun goes down, all you have are your memories to keep you warm." She spoke all of this without looking up from her rolling operation. She had clearly been listening and absorbing the random musings that I had been spouting and adopted a similar interpretation. She finished rolling and looked up at me. She continued her perspective: "So ultimately, the older we get, the more we can look back instead of forward. Each day a further reminder of all the things left unsaid, all the actions left undone, forever." She tapped the joint down on the top of her box. Her voice was gorgeous. It was like warm honey pouring into my ears. She was so very eloquent, so clear in every word she spoke. Her tone though, was searching. Like a hand that clawed in the dark, reaching for something unknown but certain it would grasp hold somewhere, somehow. She finished her commentary with a question.

"So then, Pete, when you are old and you look back on your life, are you going to write sad songs about how your best times have passed? Or will you write sad songs about the fact that the best times never came?" With her question complete she lit up, inhaled, exhaled, and looked to me for a response.

I answered with the first thing that came into my head: "I guess I'll just have to wait and see." As soon as I'd said it I cringed at myself. A philosophy student should have been able to come up with something much more compelling than that! She just shrugged. Then she took a few more puffs before she placed it down in the ash tray and passed it over to me. In the smoke I didn't even notice her lying down on the futon until the back of her head landed in my lap. I looked down and saw her eyes staring straight up at me. I didn't think anything of it; it was comfortable after all, and I had some weed to smoke, and some Floyd to listen to. All in all, I thought everything was just quite lovely.

For the next hour we didn't speak, we just lay and listened, and smoked of course. I was attaching some sort of personal significance to every note and lyric, I assumed she was doing the same. I felt an enormous amount of empathy towards her. We had spent the last sixty minutes or so involved in some sort of highly intimate activity during which neither of us spoke or really moved. It had been a beautiful time. The only thing that had occupied my mind apart from the music had been Jackie's question. But there was a simple answer in the end: *"I wouldn't write any sad songs, I wouldn't have to, I'd have B, so what would I have to be sad about?"* Nearing the mid-point of the final track of the album I moved my hand to grab my near empty pack of cigarettes. I became aware of the fact that my hand was actually resting palm-down on Jackie's cheek. I'd had no recollection of putting it there, it was just some subconscious act I must have performed whilst lost in the mental labyrinth of my mind. As the final track ended and the bells faded away, she turned sideways and faced me.

"So, what are we going to do now then Pete?"

I was slightly taken aback by the ambiguous tone of her question. *"What does she mean by that?"* I thought to myself. Before I could answer, she spoke again,

"Well, my box is empty, and I imagine B would appreciate you checking on her." I understood this phrase to be a polite invitation to leave. It had been hours since I'd seen B and I missed her. Jackie was an obviously attractive and intelligent woman, and we also had lots in common. If I had never met B I would have probably entertained the idea of having a relationship with her. That would obviously have been dependent on how she felt about me. It would have been flattering to my ego to find out that she found me as attractive as I found her, but it was a moot point. Spending that time with Jackie had been a jolly pleasant experience, but she was no B. B was the other side of my coin, the heads to my tails. Due to the woeful limitations of words and language I would never be able to properly verbalise how I felt about her to anyone, though I often tried and failed to. The only person who understood was B herself. That was because her understanding came through the eyes and not the mouth.

Whilst I had been sat thinking about B and being stoned, Jackie had gone upstairs to use the bathroom, the loud clanging of the age-old plumbing in dire contrast to the wavelike harmonies of the last hour. I stood up, managed to pull my jacket on and did up the zip. I would make my exit and leave Jackie to her own devices. There would be a hug, and some pleasantries and I would walk back to see B, germs and all. I loitered in the hallway by the door at the bottom of the stairs and waited for Jackie to come and see me off. I heard the soft thuds of her feet descending the stairs. As she crested the final step and saw me, she gave me a quizzed expression.

"What have you got your coat on for?" she asked.

"Well, you said you'd run out of weed and that I should go and check in on B, so I took that as a diplomatic cue to leave you be." It was a pretty logical deduction in my mind. She laughed.

"Ha, no, silly boy," she divulged with a grin. "I said my box was empty, that just meant I needed to fill it up from my big new bag upstairs. And I meant that you should message B and find out how she is." How in the name of sanity I was supposed to decipher that from her original statement I would never know! Jackie then squeezed past me in the narrow corridor and stopped halfway. Our heads were inches away from each other.

She spoke sweetly and softly,

"You can go if you want to. But I've got lots more weed here and lots more music to listen to." It sounded to me as though she was actively encouraging me to stay. It was exceedingly tempting. Smoke some more, listen some more, talk some more with a friend. She pushed all the way past me and went back to the lounge. As she sat, she pulled out a plastic bag full of green buds. She tapped her fingers rhythmically on the bag.

"Well?" she posed. I hesitated with my response.

"I really should go and see how B is doing."

I got a quick, "Okay fine," delivered back to me. She stood up and went to escort me to the door. She seemed a little hurt that I didn't want to stay with her. I put my hands out and spoke again before she'd taken two steps.

"I *should* go and see how B is, but … I'm not going to let you smoke all of that by yourself."

Jackie grinned at me showing the full force of her flawless smile. I unzipped my jacket and slid it off my shoulders. I re-slung it over the chair.

I lost B when I took off that jacket.

{Chapter 0 cont.}

|Take a Breath|

I feel another brisk surge of wind wisp through my hair. From the commotion behind me I assess that the gawping crowd has swelled a little. I'm also aware that the police have stopped all traffic from crossing the bridge. It wasn't my intention to inconvenience anyone's day. I am just doing things the way I want to do them, for the first time in years. I feel a sense of liberty at the sensation. I'm doing things the way *I* want to do them. It's a good feeling. I must have been standing here for about half an hour or so by now. Time flies when you're having fun! The rushing water below looks ready for me. I take a breath and steady myself, blocking out all of the external detritus.

I force my mind to push past the wretched memory of taking my jacket off; the sight in my mind's eye of that futon. For nearly twenty years that memory has hurt me. That action of taking my jacket off was probably the most pivotal and destructive of my life. That moment could have gone either way. The deadly cocktail of youth, hubris and ego combined to see my jacket unzipped and rehung. I have never stopped paying for it, never stopped regretting it. So many times I have wished I had played that night differently. Wished I had just said my goodbyes and left. Gone back to check on B, gone back to my room, gone anywhere.

The years since have been one long fantasy about what could have happened had I just gone out the door that night, with my jacket on. Every chance I'd had to compose my thoughts, I'd imagined years of happiness. Years of holiday adventures and shared experiences. Years with B. Being able to see her smile every morning of every day, even as the first grey hairs started to penetrate our scalps. Several times a day I'd disappear behind my eyes and exist in that reality, but I always knew it was a lie. No matter how hard I tried to convince myself I could exist there, I'd always have to open my eyes and deal with real life.

More than once I'd hoped for insanity to claim me, to lose all rational sense of reality and dwell in delusion forever, but I wasn't that lucky. Alas, my alarmingly functional mind dissolved that fateful evening down to two points.

One: I should not have taken my jacket off.

Two: no matter how hard I yearned to go back in time and fix it, I couldn't.

In the intervening years since then I'd often say aloud to myself, "You can't go back." It was a statement I was never incorrect in saying. You really can't go back, well, not in this world anyway.

I force my memory past the grief, force it past the point of no return. Force it forward, to truth, and to tears.

{Chapter 20}

|White Grass|

I stayed, Jackie rolled, we smoked. We smoked together; it was weird stuff. We swiftly adopted our previous positions on her futon. Her body felt lusciously warm, the heat transition from her to me felt like the most exquisite radiator known to man. As far as the music went, I had asked for another Pink Floyd album. She commented,

"The last one was your choice, now it's my turn."

She sat up away from me quicker than she had placed herself down. She reached back into her CD collection and plucked out a rather unusually modern and alternative record. And so, we lit up and blazed away to the sound of 'The MUSIC's' second album, 'Welcome to the North'. I was unfamiliar with it but I had enjoyed their eponymously titled debut album. The distorted, modern tones were a sharp counter to the softened mellow harmonies of the Floyd. Both were music filled with feeling, but this purveyed more of a raw passion as compared to the measured restraint of Pink.

The stuff we were smoking out of the new bag was not the same as the smooth bud from her previous boxed supply. After the first joint I felt distinctly unusual. It was like being extremely drunk and stoned simultaneously, with an added feeling of artificial invulnerability. By the time the album had reached track four, Jackie had managed to completely curl and twine her body around mine. I could perceive her natural scent saturating me, and I liked it. Her long hair tickled seductively against the skin of my bare forearm. I could feel her entire body pulsating with feminine rhythm to the deep beat of the projected baseline, a pulse that gyrated against me with indecorous temptation. Her eyes were closed but she mouthed along to most of the youthful lyrics. She licked her lips between some of the vocal pauses, and I knew that she knew I could see her doing it.

Between the next tracks she sat up and reached for her rolling apparatus. She rolled silently, filling the paper with whatever substance it was that was in that new bag. She finished the roll and puffed away callously. When it came to my turn, she insisted that she be the one to hold it whilst I partook. She knelt over me, straddled me over the futon and grinned as she pressed the joint to my lips. I could feel warmth and pressure from the side of her fingers as she held it to my mouth. I drew it in, I blew it out, I felt exalted. She repeated the sequence several more times, and with each dire repetition I felt my mental capacity drain away, replaced with inane stupefaction. Although my more accurate senses had blurred to a smear, I could still feel her warmth. Her heat seemed to exacerbate with every breath. Whatever it was I was smoking it was certainly making its pungent effects known. My brain was a whirlwind of hazed passion and misplaced ego. Lost inside the music, lost inside the situation, lost to the basest foundation of the masculine mind.

I couldn't pin-point an exact moment when we were both naked, but it certainly happened at some point. Her satin soft lips and slick tongue caressed my own as she locked her supple legs around my spine. Her hips pounded atop me like pistons from a burning engine, her palms pressed down on both my shoulders. The pale blue light of pre-dawn filtered in through the thin curtains. Beads of cold sweat fell from her chest onto mine; her essence permeated my cells. Her panting was distant, like an echo in an unsolicited dream. I climaxed in a state of chemically-fuelled anxious ambivalence. My final semi-lucid memory of the event was feeling Jackie climb off me. She kissed me on my brow, then disappeared upstairs. My eyelids fell and darkness took me, entirely.

{Chapter 21}

|Going Back|

I got out the car and stood tall and true. I felt the keening of the wind against my face, razor cold and honest. It had been more than fifteen years since I'd last laid eyes upon the wet stone and lush green of this place. Unfettered waves of forgotten butterflies laced my existence with the unanswered potential of an unfinished, broken road. I inhaled deeply. I hoped that the ambient air would transport me back to better days. I wanted to turn back time, to turn back those years of disappointment, depression and regret. I shut my eyes as tightly as nature would allow; nature replied with further cold breeze, and rain. As I opened my eyes, I tried to force a superimposed image of the past onto them. I wanted to hallucinate, to see it how it was in the past; I tried to force away my stubborn sanity. I had hoped that somehow just by the mere act of returning that it would have cracked my rational mind into a million shards that all existed in the past, but it hadn't. Tried though I did, all I could see was the rain, the wet cars driving past, and the odd umbrella on the High Street. I locked the car and began a slow and ponderous march through the streets of my youth, an emotional tour down the avenues of yesteryear.

I stopped and found myself staring at a bench. The intensity of the rain increased a little. I stood with the resolve of an eroded statue. To any passing onlookers I must have seemed quite odd. A thirty-something figure stood motionless in front of a bench in the pouring rain was surely not a common sight in any town. But this wasn't any old bench, this was the bench that a young man once sat on, reading Wordsworth and musing on his future. A boy who despite his supposed knowledge, didn't know a thing.

"What would I say to him if I could go back and talk to him? What would I say?"

I imagined my younger version sitting in optimistic isolation. I sat down next to him, the wet bench soaked through my clothes and into my skin. I braced for a conversation with my younger self.

"Hello."

"Hello," came my clean voice with a youthful naivety. Even to think of myself speaking with such innocence brought a lump to my throat.

"I am you from the future, I have so many things to tell you."

"Oh really, go on then."

"Well, firstly, I think it's paramount that you don't become me."

"Oh that's fine, I don't intend to," my junior self proclaimed with passive indolence.

"Neither did I," I warned as I laughed out of my nose and gently sprayed some of the rainwater away from my face. I continued to give the benefit of my years to my fledgling incarnation.

"So, this year, you're going to start off really well. You are going to fall in love with the most perfect and beautiful entity ever to grace this earth, and she will love you too. Then you will fall in with a bad crowd of artificial friends, you'll take too many drugs, and by the time you leave this place after your first year you'll be a mental and emotional cluster fuck!"

"That doesn't sound like me," the boyish me muttered dismissively.

"Huh, not yet perhaps, but trust me, if you make all those same bad choices then you are going to cause us a wagon-load of heartache and regret." In my time since Llantarn I hadn't spoken with such sincerity and gusto, yet when faced with my younger shadow I found the words and meaning that had escaped me for so long. Life is such a ludicrous design.

"Are you sure you're me from the future? Because you are using the same tone that my father uses when he talks to me."

"Never mind my tone! Have you actually listened to a single word I've said?"

"Yes. But I surely can't change anything that's going to happen, can I? I mean, if you really are me from the future then I am destined to grow into you. I have to make all the mistakes that you've made in order to know that they were mistakes. If I don't err in such a seemingly grievous manner then I could never become you. I could never sit next to my past self and warn him about his future. I am you, and you are me. We can't go back."

"Ha!" I exclaimed. "That's the truth isn't it. That's the bloody truth." I looked at my feet, my shoes sodden with the persistent flow of rainwater. "The bloody truth," I resigned again. I turned my head to gaze upon my youthful features, the tight and unjaded skin. There was only an empty bench on an empty street.

I picked myself up off the bench and strolled on through the rain. Every pace was another step down memory lane. The town had changed. High Street retail names were brazenly brandished where once local retailers had been. Several of the pubs of my day were shut up and boarded over. It was thoroughly depressing. The streets had lost the unique charm of my time, replaced with a cut, copy and paste.

I rounded a corner and saw a group of students walking toward me. They were robed in the drab garbs of Topshop and River Island, no sight of spectral colours or patchwork cloth. Their tops were considerably oversized for their torsos and their jeans significantly too tight. A couple of them wore university branded hoodies. The type of hoodie that had been mass produced in sweat shops and printed on at the end with the name of whatever establishment required an order. Every other university sold them in my day, but not Llantarn. That was probably due to the nature of the typical Llantarn student, as unique as the campus. The notion that all these individuals would voluntarily buy what was essentially a uniform made no logical sense. It clearly made no financial sense either as the university shop never sold them. When I was here it was a statement of pride to wear a hoodie that was handmade, distinct and individual. Something that bore several yin-yang symbols, along with an ohm or two. The students progressing before me were clearly in the feral grips of sobriety. There were no deformed gaits of drunkenness or random diagonal stagger of drugs. My depression sank further. As they passed by me, I heard one of them pronounce something about "Jean-Paul Sartre" in a preposterously pretentious accent. It filled me with jealousy and rage. The jealousy was obviously due to the fact that I wished I was young again and part of a student cohort. The rage was - well, it was rage by proxy. I had spent the best part of two decades in the company of people who were generally not fans of students. I guessed that some of their hatred and intolerance had seeped into my psyche through communal osmosis. I had heard many a rant and rave come from people on the topic of students, especially on my evenings sat in 'The Anchor and Axe'. A splinter of that bitter callousness had clearly metastasised inside me to some degree. I didn't like that reality, but I guess I'm just the combined bitch of Darwin and Freud. As they passed me by and the physical distance between us grew, I felt the jealousy and rage fall away.

My rational senses took over and I walked into the foyer of 'The White Lion' to check-in and get my room. It was this hotel which would serve as my temporary sanctuary for the next couple of days. I eventually had my key issued to me by the mental underachiever who had been employed to work at reception. After claiming several times that I didn't have a reservation, he asked how I was spelling my surname. I spelled it out for him in no uncertain terms: "M-O-R-G-A-N." I made no disguise of my irritation with my tired and wet tone.

"Oh, yeah, I see the problem, I was searching for a booking with the name Mor*gen.*"

Only in Wales could you get a concierge confused with the name Morgan!

'The White Lion' was always regarded as the most up-market place in town. I remembered that the food was good. I remembered B and me eating in the restaurant more than once. I remembered how a student loan could make you feel like a king. A powerful king. A younger version of me had once examined that feeling and framed it into a question; *what is power?* Just one of the many intriguing questions I hadn't asked myself for such a long time.

As I entered my room, I noticed that I had been given room one hundred and one. Room 101. The implications of the number were not lost on me, in fact, I'd thought it somehow fitting. Since leaving Llantarn I had wished on more than one occasion that I was Winston.

I took off my soaked clothes and lay naked upon the bed. I considered the question that I had not pondered in many years. I even spoke it aloud to myself: "What is power?" I continued aloud to myself in the empty room. "Is power something external? A permission given to you, with, or without your knowledge? Is power something that has to be earned through knowledge and experience? Is power simply the ability and capability to affect things in some way?"

As I spoke to myself it became impossible to voice all of the notions that I had triggered in my mind. A myriad of postulates rained down upon my thoughts as kinetic as the rain that fell outside. I stared into space. Ultimately, only one thought took precedence; only one thought reverberated through my process.

"The only true power extant in an individual is the power to distinguish between internal happiness and sadness."

I sat up on my loaned bed, my definition of power ringing inside my skull. I was happy with my conclusion. And after all, the only person I had to justify my resolutions to was myself. I shook off my mental musings and started to prepare myself for more immediate and physical issues. The reason I had come back. It was not to tease myself with what could have been, nor to commune with myself regarding the nature of power. I had come back to try and reconnect. To try and relive all those nights when true love had seemed possible. I dabbed myself down with one of the hotel towels and dressed my body adequately. I grabbed my phone, my keys, my wallet, my cigarettes and my courage, and I left the room and headed out for 'The Royal Ivy'.

{Chapter 22}
|Unreal Unity|

I was pleasantly, nay, vigorously surprised to find that 'The Royal Ivy' was exactly how it had been back in the days I remembered, back in the days I clung to. It was as though the intervening years had never occurred. The dart board was still slung surrounded by the same old tyre, the bar itself still bore the dents and tales of the previous century, the previous millennium. I found it comforting that amongst all the apparent change there still existed at least one solid vestibule of consistency. I ordered a pint and took station in a quiet corner. I quickly stood up from it and repositioned myself to the place that B and I had first met. Perhaps it would trigger a sub-layer in her consciousness when she arrived. Probably not but I'd take any edge I could get. I had been extremely surprised to hear from her, though I had kept my mobile number the same since university just in case she should try and get in touch. It was a tactic that had clearly paid dividends. I was beyond nervous. I was like a child at Christmas. I could hardly even drink my drink. Anxious sipping was the best I could manage as I rapidly tapped my foot on the floor. As my foot tapped away furiously, I managed to find some mental respite by getting lost in my thoughts.

I was entombed in a crypt of internal monologue. A state I had become woefully comfortable with over the years. I'd use my interior arena as a crucible for forging ideas and analysing where it all went wrong, then keep all conclusions to myself.

What's the real difference between nostalgia and regret? When we look back on the long shadows of our past selves, do we really wish we could change things? Wish we had been more mature, more reasoned, more strategic with our choices? Or is it the case that our latent self convinces us that it was the unbridled emotions of youth that caused all current lack of lifestyle fulfilment? Do we think that in order to deflect our thoughts away from the real horror? The terrible truth that the way we lived in our adolescence was the *real* mode in which to live. That the way in which society has since trained us to exist is in fact a lie. The way full adulthood forces concepts upon us is just an engineered trap to keep us away from the feeling of real autonomy. A construct that narrows the choices of freedom down to practical necessities of survival; a protracted slow-motion suicide. A plot that makes adopting adulthood the only option left to take. That's the difference. Nostalgia is remembering the feeling of having the choice to carve your own discrete but dangerous path; regret is knowing you took the same perfunctory path as everyone else. Nostalgia is missing the feeling of not having to make choices. Regret is the feeling of having made them. By the time anyone examines this issue with any significant pursuit it is already too late - they are already neck deep in mortgage payments, tax rebates and parking disputes. Rather than confront the hilarious irrelevance of what they are doing, they pass social media judgements on those who dare to not do the same. Mature society is so far removed from endorsing the incompliant that it chokes itself in a security of infinite fallacy. The fashions of social justice prevail over any honest analysis. Who *really* cares anymore for the flowers in the hair, or the bleeding hearts of artists? Just so long as there are trendy hats on guitar stands with politically correct posters on the background wall. Drama for the sake of drama. Drugs for the sake of drugs. Candy canes and mandarins in a smoke filtered scene. Plastic cleavage with fake smiles for a 'like' in the land of perpetual now. Shirts, ties and pleasant smiles for placid passive enemies. The worst part being the fact that I am a part of it all, just another dead leaf trying to cling onto a branch of the money tree. But not today. Today, I'd see her again.

She was always so perfect. So perfect in her multitude of perfections. To try and describe her to someone was like trying to describe the sounds of jazz to a deaf man. Even to try was as futile as trying to ice skate up the face of Everest. The day I received her message I felt a primordial surge of euphoria. I was entangled within the pixels on my phone that read, "1 New Message – B"

The content of it had merely been, "Hey," but my heart skipped a dozen beats and my mind flooded with notions of reconciliation and re-joining. After a textual conversation it transpired that she wanted to meet me. I had obviously acquiesced to her request. She had no concept of what it would mean to me just to see her again. She had made it abundantly clear in her messages that she was happy with her current partner but she wanted to see me regardless. I didn't care in the slightest about her motivations for meeting me or for her supposed relationship bliss. All that factored in my mind was the idea of being able to physically see her again, in the flesh. For the first time in so many years I might actually remember what it was like to feel alive, even if it was only for a day, even for just an hour.

We had agreed to meet at five o'clock, so I was a bit early. An entire hour early. Still, I'd rather be an hour early for this than one second late. I ran through all the things I would say to her, played out multiple scenarios of how I would react when she'd walk through the door. Every hypothetical line I drew in my mind made me doubt that she would actually come. The rest of the pub was empty, so at least if this was some sort of mentally abortive manifestation then it wouldn't have to be played out in front of any unsuspecting parties. I tried to calm down; I drank more freely from my pint glass and my foot slowly stopped tapping. There was still quite a gulf in time before she was supposed to arrive. The more I drank, the quicker the time passed, but each time I heard the sound of a door banging, I leapt out of my skin, leapt out of my soul. I had a cigarette roughly every ten minutes, the hassle of having to go outside now forcibly integrated into the smoking experience. At least it had stopped raining. I was half concerned and half hopeful that whilst I was stood outside I would be able to see her coming. I didn't. I stubbed out another cigarette and went back inside. It was half-past four, thirty minutes to go. I got a message on my phone, it was from B.

"Hey, can you come to the patio of The King's Head instead?"

Of course I had no objection. I'd just got a fresh pint in but I left it as though it didn't exist. As soon as I set foot outside the pub I had to smoke again. It was far more nerve racking to walk to a place where she already was. But all the nerves in the world weren't going to stop me from seeing her again. That's all I really wanted. Just to see her, see her with my own eyes. If I could just see her then I'd know. I'd know that happiness was still possible. In spite of all the odds and all the past, there was still a chance for us to be happy together. As long as she was alive and as long as I was alive, the chance existed. That chance was all I needed to carry on with life. So, I walked. I walked to the end of the street on which 'The Royal Ivy' was set, and turned onto the street where 'The King's Head' was. Originally, she had wanted to meet in London. I didn't know why, but had guessed it was an attempt at complete anonymity. I would have gone to London to see her, I would have gone to hell to see her, but I thought I'd chance my arm in the hope of nostalgic reunion. I had managed to switch the meeting place to Llantarn. Now, only a few paces away from her I could feel my heart beat like a spasmodic clock and my blood pressure was as stable as a medieval monarchy. I had to press through it, press through it all. The ultimate prize of seeing her again was far too valuable to ruin with internal fear. I had decided to just look at the pavement until I got to the pub patio. It was by far the safest strategy. I had no idea how I would cope with seeing her blurry outline come into focus. I'd much rather just be hit with it in a single volley. So I walked swiftly with my head down. It wasn't long before I was there. And there she was.

She looked up at me and smiled. She stood up from the table and wrapped her arms around me. Naturally I responded in kind. She was real. I could have died in that second. I could have passed away fulfilled then and there without us even exchanging a word, but that wasn't to be. She spoke and I was treated to her husky angelic tones for the first time in so many dark days.

"Hey." Her single syllable was an orgasmic symphony to me. She said no more but let go of our embrace and sat back down. Though it pained me beyond measure to let her go I followed suit. We sat opposite each other over the patio table. All I could get out in the form of a verbal reply was to mimic her word.

"Hey." I barely managed to echo back to her.

She had never seemed so nebulous and yet so real. She exhaled gently out of her nose whilst slightly twisting her head. I remembered her doing that when she was thinking.

Whilst I sat in front of her there was only one thing I could reasonably do, smoke. She was already smoking a roll-up so for at least an entire minute we just smoked and looked at each other. I felt like she was examining me; all I could do was fight back the tears and try and maintain a stoic visage. One of us had to break the silence, and I decided it would be me.

"So…" Yeah, what a triumph of sparkling conversation that was.

"So," she replied with effortless grace. I had a plethora of questions to ask her, but I didn't feel like I could ask any of them straight away. I couldn't think of any bullshit chit chat either. She just sat there, perfect, smoking, and watching. I had to say or do something more. I asked a question that I really wanted to know the answer to, but probably could have asked with a bit more tact.

"Did you come down here alone or is your boyfriend with you?" I blurted out. Regardless of the crudity that I had employed it left her in no doubt as to the question itself.

"I'm alone," she said, which made my heart sing. I thought, *"Maybe she hasn't even told him that she's come here."* I had to press the issue.

"So what did Roy say when you told him you were coming here? I can't imagine he was very happy about it."

She answered without hesitation or deceit. "Roy doesn't know that I'm here."

It was as though all my prayers had been answered. B, a person whose honesty I had never known to be swayed, had lied to her partner. Not only lied to him, she had lied to him and also met me. I tried to camouflage my reaction and restrained my response to, "I see." I tried to make my two words seem as unjudgmental as possible. One whiff of sanctimonious sentiment and B would have run for the hills. She just looked at me, inhaled her cigarette and extended her hand with fingers splayed. I responded with mirrored action and our palms joined, our fingers clasped. I had to dig so horribly deep to avoid crying. I managed to avert tears, but it would be a while before I could speak properly without my voice noticeably shaking.

"Why, Pete?" she asked. Fuck me! What a question. Considering the multiple avenues that question could descend down I asked for some clarity.

"Why what? Why what in particular?"

B shuffled a little but still kept a tight grasp of my hand.

"Why didn't you tell me the first time?" she asked as she stared searchingly at me. I was too ashamed to meet her gaze.

"I couldn't," I forced out with my eyes now fixed upon the concrete floor. I could have given a decent load of excuses why I didn't. Excuses like drugs, stupidity, gullibility, but none of those was a reasonable explanation. I forced my gaze up ninety degrees. I carried on.

"The real reason is quite simple. I was a coward."

B tightened her grip on my hand.

"Pete, with what you've been through since then, I know you're not a coward."

"B, there's more than one kind of coward. When it comes to you, I am all of them and more. I was so afraid of losing you that I couldn't tell you. Jackie knew that."

"So you're blaming Jackie, are you?" she asked.

"No, no, not at all. I was the one who stayed there. I was the one that fucked up." I had fucked up, that was for sure.

"Why didn't you tell me as soon as it happened?"

"Hence you see the cowardice."

"But why keep going back to her? I mean, you must have liked her enough on some level."

"I kept going back because if I hadn't, she'd have told you about everything herself. I couldn't cope with that, I couldn't cope with losing you."

"So, you kept fucking another woman to avoid losing the woman you were in love with?"

Wow, what an impossible question.

"Yes." That was all I could say. It was the truth, a retarded masculine truth, but truth nonetheless. Throughout the exchange so far, B had not let go of my hand. I could only interpret that as a good sign.

"It would have been better to hear it from you rather than from Jayne. I was so utterly humiliated by the whole experience; I don't think you can understand," she lamented.

I responded, "Maybe I didn't feel the humiliation, but I am the one who has had to live with the knowledge of what I have done for the last God knows how many years. In some ways I think it is easier to be a victim than a genuinely remorseful criminal. Because you know what, you can't go back. You just can't go back." After my little speech I expected B to pull her hand away and disappear off into the Welsh ether. She didn't.

Instead, she merely insisted, "Pete, you were a cunt. Jackie was also a cunt."

And with that statement it was like she had wiped away all the years of hurt, all the years of despair. It was like forgiveness wrapped inside a punch that I was more than willing to take. She still held my hand. She had brought me back from the brink of endless regret to a state of hope. But I still had questions for her. I asked,

"So, B, why didn't you tell Roy about you coming here?"

All I got was silence in return. I tried asking in a different way.

"So, what *did* you tell Roy about where you were going?"

She didn't elaborate on exactly what she had told him. She only stated,

"He knows I'll be away from home for a few days." I couldn't really force the issue anymore at that point. I decided to leave it alone and perhaps circle back to it later.

For the rest of the day, B and I got reacquainted. I told her about the thesis I had developed since leaving Llantarn. She wasn't very impressed by it, but that didn't matter. We caught up with the last decade and more of separation. Neither of us had kept up communications with anyone from university, so we drank and mused upon the hypothetical lives of people we once knew. Her eyes warmed with conversation that remembered all of the days spent in bed together, smoking and watching films. We spoke of the glory of the past summer sun, and as the memories were vocalised, we both reminisced about just how fantastic it really was and how grateful we both were to have taken part in the freeing madness of it all. The absence of responsibility, the feeling of youthful energy that prevailed over the forces of conformity and continuity. It was as though the years of separation had fallen away and it was just me and her, just the two us. Every cell in my body felt alive and alert, as if I had been cleansed of the past, and in the present I was born anew.

There were some films, some books, some passages of text I had come across in my life: powerful, visceral moments of connection or abstraction. Moments I wished I could forget just so I could experience them again for the first time. That time I spent with B was as though my soul had found a reset and I could feel all those things again - I could knock down all the walls I had built through her eyes; I could unlock any emotional bastion with the way her sweet smile made me feel. There was no pain anymore. The chimes of the bell of time had no power over us. It was an electric eclipse of nature.

She had a room booked in 'The White Lion' as well, on the first night she had invited me to leave her room in the small hours and cold light of early morning. She was tired from her journey and subsequent alcohol consumption, and in truth so was I. I kissed her on her forehead and went back to my own room. I managed to get off to sleep eventually, after I had stopped smiling at the ceiling.

The next morning, I awoke and sent her a text which asked her to message me when she was up. I didn't want to disturb her sleep by knocking on her door too early. Instead, I got up and decided to go for a personal amble around the campus, a stroll around my old haunts, a tour through my youth. It was the most underwhelming expedition of my life. I wanted to see good old Hawson Hall. I could never forget the aroma of the place, as all buildings have their own unique smell. Although I could remember it in some corner of my mind it would be nothing like being able to inhale it once again in the flesh. Smell could trigger such evocative memories. I was fully ready and excited to unlock some of those memories just by walking in and being hit by the fragrance of past adventures.

When I arrived at the main Hawson door I was completely disheartened to find that I couldn't open it. There was a small black box next to the door which was explicitly for the use of authorised personnel to press an approved fob to in order to gain access. I had no such key, so I had to leave the lid on the box of all the memories I had hoped to internally unveil. The thought of needing some form of technology to gain access to a hall on campus was totally Orwellian. It was the complete antithesis of what the university social life had stood for back in my day. Further to the secure access terminal, there was another addition to the architecture of the building: a closed-circuit security camera that faced directly down upon the main entrance. All the feelings I had had when I first arrived here as a teenager felt violated. Freedom of movement was now controlled and all comings and goings monitored. It felt less like a campus and more like a prison. I unsuccessfully fought back a tear. I sat on top of the bike hut in front of the hall and just looked at what the place had become as a cold tear rolled down my cheek. Centuries of anonymity and exploration dissolved into a camera screen in an office of observation. I had to smoke.

I took myself down from my lofty perch and walked around some more. On every hall there was an access box and accompanying camera. Fucking Nazis! It was past eleven and still no message from B. I decided to go to the union bar and see what had become of that. I was met with another black fob security box. Clearly the union building was now a tightly controlled area. There were also at least four cameras dotted about the complex that I could see. *"What were they for? Was the current student populace so afraid of the people from town potentially invading them?"* I just didn't understand, but I wasn't going to give up on gaining access. I had had some of the greatest sessions of my life in that building, and I would find a way to get in and see those walls once again. My time in the military had given me a basic understanding of social engineering, though I had never tried to employ it in a real-life scenario. It was just like bluffing at poker. You had to be so genuine that it would leave people in no doubt as to the reason why you were doing what you were doing. I knew that at some point soon a student would come along and beep their way into the building, and that would be my opportunity. I would make up some bullshit lie as to why they needed to buzz me in too and they would do it, because that's how humans in the western world are programmed to behave. Till then I only had two things to do: think of a lie to tell, and smoke. *"What should I lie about?"* I looked like a normal male: jeans, a couple of days of razor stubble, un-styled hair. *"What could I say that would be plausible and unsuspecting?"* I considered my appearance and wondered if I could get away with it. *"Could I really claim to just be a student who had forgotten his fob?"* If I said it with a sufficiently earnest voice then I was sure it would work. After all, it wasn't as though there would be a constant stream of people trying to gain nefarious access into the complex. It was a Students' Union, not a bank vault or secret bunker.

So, I just sat on one the tables out in front of the entrance and waited. I smoked and saw several warning signs plastered on the walls and windows. "BEWARE - The Students' Union is under CONSTANT SURVEILLANCE" read one alert which was shown in Welsh as well. I wondered about the cost of putting such interrogative technology around all the Army, Navy and RAF barracks and bars. It would have been colossal. Yet the current university management had seen fit to spend the money to implement such a system here. It was a truly pathetic state of affairs. *Mae Big Brother yn eich gwylio chi.* I waited. I didn't have to wait long. A young lad with long hair and a meek face came to the door and pressed his key to the access box, I sprang into action and followed tightly behind him. He turned his head and saw me.

"Hey, sorry, mind if I piggy back on you? I left my key in my room," I hustled with a positive tone. All he did was shrug. That was that, I was inside. He disappeared off up the main stairs without giving me a second thought and I was left alone, stood in the small entrance hall of the building. The colours on the walls had changed, the framed posters were long gone, but the smell - the smell was the same. I breathed it in deeply, and I remembered. I remembered carrying Wozza outside so he could be sick; I remembered Ste carrying me outside so I could be sick; I remembered being inebriated and young. It made me smile. I walked on into the bar: it was distinctly different.

The stools, tables, even the walls had changed. It was not somewhere I recognised. The windows at least hadn't changed, so all of the natural light patterns that fell were the same, but what they fell on was alien. I couldn't stand it for more than a minute. I couldn't stand this new image attempting to superimpose itself onto my cherished memories so I turned and ran. My Llantarn was gone. At least I didn't have to face it alone. As I stormed out in a pathos-fuelled fury my phone chimed with a message from B. Within minutes I would be with her again and all the grief would be forgotten, or at least shared.

We went to brunch together in the hotel. We had planned to go to 'Wynn's Diner', but unfortunately Wynn had died. His café was boarded up, and there was a rumour that it might become a 'Café Nero'. I told B about my morning's reconnaissance. I told her that she would have to see it to believe it.

"Seriously, you need special keys just to go from one hall to another, and you're always being watched!" She understood every word I had said, and because of that she chose to not go anywhere near the campus.

"My memories of being a student here and feeling the way I felt are so unexplainably precious that I don't want to see what it has become. It would be like going back to an art gallery that housed your favourite painting and gushing spray paint all over it."

She was such a wordsmith. I had always loved that about her; I loved everything about her. The rest of that day was spent in the beer garden of 'The King's Head'. One of the fragile locales that, like 'The Royal Ivy', had escaped alteration over the years. We spoke about how the pair of us were the real masters of space and time, and that the only power the universe has is the power that we give it. Unfortunately, the tunes of fate caught us up. The next morning, she had to leave, and so did I. The notion of descending back into reality was vomit inducing. The cruel mistress of time marched ever on, and we had to accept that one more evening was all we had.

We were in the restaurant of 'The White Lion'. We had laughed and smiled through the meal, chuckled and giggled through our drinks. After the dessert plates had been removed, we were faced with the reality of a dawn departure. As much as we might have wished, we could not escape it. The bell finally caught up with us as it rang out to call time at the bar. As it did our microclimate developed an air of seriousness. I faced it directly.

"So, what about tomorrow?" I asked with a hopeful resignation.

"Well, I will drive away, and so will you," she answered. She understood that I had meant much more in my question than the next day's logistics, but she clearly didn't want to broach the topic. I did.

"What about the day after tomorrow?" I asked in order to press the real meaning of my first question. I could sense that she didn't want to answer. The majority of me didn't want her to answer either.

In my dream world she would say, *"I will go home and tell Roy that I am still in love with you. We will break up; I will move out of our place and move in with you. We will find a way to make it work, we will be together."*

But she was never going to say that. What she actually replied with was, "We will both go back to our lives and be grateful that we had this time together again. We will fulfil our obligations and maybe one day we will be able to do it again."

She saw my physical distress at her answer. I couldn't have hoped to have hidden it. She spoke again, more softly and sultrily. "Why don't you focus on tonight before you start to worry about tomorrow?"

Half an hour or so later we were both in her room. My heart pounded like a virgin's. She lay on the bed and I lay down beside her. When we kissed it was just like the first kiss. Not like the first kiss with her, but the first kiss of my life. Her lips were a complex fabric of narcotic silk and her tongue a laden quill of sensation. Her eyes, oh, her eyes! They were dark supernovas of intimacy and lust.

As we disrobed each other and pressed our two bodies into one, all the lies of life, the universe, and everything were debunked. There was just us. Hurricanes of passion swirled inside our veins. Any perception of borders or boundaries were laid low in the face of our conjoined essence, our symbiotic energy. Separation: nothing more than a transcended convention. Our physical union mirrored in the spiritual one, whatever or wherever that may be. Our breaths were as one, our pulses pounded in unison. Our movements were instantly reciprocated with perfect counterpoint. Poets, authors and orchestras could only hope to relay a pale facsimile of the harmonious perfection that we achieved that night. Pores in both our skins let loose sweat just so it could mix together and combine into some mystic solution. A joint crescendo of emotion and appetite consumed us, a build-up of metaphysical proportions. Both our breathing quickened in sympathy. Nails raked across my back and drew willing crimson as my teeth cut into her tender shoulder. We bled together under the crystal Welsh stars where we had first met. It wasn't violence, it was sacred nature in all its honesty. Our eyes locked together when the moment came; we existed in a state of hyper-consciousness where all points in our lives were instantaneously connected.

Then it was over. Then there was just sleep. And that sleep brought unlaboured peace. It was the total absence of consciousnesses. It was a peace that the most pious of men could only imagine. A homogenous darkness and painless abyss that was more of a home than any fireplace or front door could've ever hoped to be. I had felt the feeling before.

Songbirds and sunshine broke rudely through the curtains and woke us both. Gone were the angels of harmony and the lustful demons of satisfaction. B was nervous, anxious. She was not in the mood for cuddling. She rolled out of the bed and began to dress herself. Garbed only in a white bed sheet with red stains, I rolled over too.

"Hey, what's the problem? Why the rush?" I asked, with a happy yet sympathetic tone.

"Oh come on. You know why I feel like this."

I did. "Roy?"

"Yes, fucking Roy!" she expelled.

She not only got dressed but started to pack all of her things away. I found her compulsion to be worrying.

"Hey, calm down, we've got plenty of time before we need to be on the road," I stated softly in an attempted reassuring manner. B wasn't having any of it. She just kept putting things away and zipping up compartments on her bags. I didn't know what to do for the best, but I knew that doing nothing would solve nothing. When she was folding some of her clothes on the bed, I grabbed her tightly by both of her wrists and stopped the packing frenzy. She looked at me; I looked at her. I begged her, "Talk to me."

She did.

"I came here as a nostalgic escape. I just wanted to get away from reality for a couple of days. At least forty-eight hours without bills or anything else from real life. I had looked forward to berating you and then recounting some forgotten stories. I did not come here to have sex with you or to end my relationship."

"But you did have sex with me," I retorted without malice, just as an observation. "It was fantastic paradigm-shifting sex. Sex that could only take place between -"

She cut me off.

"Yes! The sex was phenomenal, almost paranormal, but I have a life at home, and so do you. Those webs do not interconnect at any point. So we just need to accept the realities of life and go on as normal, but with gratitude for what we have given each other here."

"Gratitude?" I shouted.

"Yes, let's just both be grateful that we have had this experience and move on for now."

"B, I still love you. I never stopped."

"Pete, I never stopped loving you either, despite all that stuff with Jackie. But this isn't about love, this is about life. I have spent years building a good one with Roy. He might not set my sweat aflame but he is a solid rock upon which I have built my life. And I need to get back to him."

"You going to tell him where you have been? Are you going to confess to him about last night?"

She stopped and thought.

"I don't know," was what she uttered. That poked a fire of hope inside me that she *would* tell him, that they would split and it would be the right time for Pete and B, Mk II. She had gathered all of her things together. I was still naked on the bed, wrapped in the bedsheet that bore the scars of the previous night. It was obvious she wanted to leave immediately. There was nothing I could do to change her mind, so I decided to endorse her departure. My heart was shattering at the idea of her leaving, but I drew on that Battle of Britain spirit to just kiss her once as she leant in to say goodbye. I used all of my remaining strength to keep a staunch stiff upper lip as she left the room. As the door to the room closed behind her my lip trembled and I cried. It was back to the dull grey tones of reality for me. Not to mention an eight-hour drive with a hangover. I had vibrated on only positive frequencies for the last two days, but now it was time for pain, despair and laborious mediocrity to take hold once more.

I settled my account with 'The White Lion' and got into my car. Such a dichotomy of feelings persisted inside me. I didn't want to go, but I couldn't stay. Llantarn was not the place it once was. But B was the same. I loved her, so I loved the place, but I had to go, urgh, there was too much confusion. The real world was pressing: time and responsibility crushed down on me from all angles. I started my engine and began the long trek north.

It was dark and cold by the time I arrived back in Scotland. It was almost nice to be home, almost, but not quite. I parked up and went in through the front door. I saw my wife stood there with a smile as our children ran toward me in their Sonic the Hedgehog pyjamas. I was back at what passed for home.

{Chapter 23}

|Homestead Horror|

I'd met Ruby not long after leaving Llantarn. She was pleasant enough to begin with. She had a pretty face, with pretty eyes and a pretty smile. She wasn't the academic sort, wasn't blessed with a high level of intellectual creativity, but at least she wasn't a total moron. Indeed, she had virtually no common understanding of politics, history, geography, science or the arts, but the sex was decent enough and her general company was initially unoffensive.

After I'd left Llantarn at the end of my first, and only, year at university, I was a wreck. I dwelt constantly on my actions and words. I longed for B. I reran the entire shit-show through my thoughts over and over. I tried to examine the whole mess, the tears, the heartache, the cruelty. I'd also had the complete ignominy and humiliation of telling my parents that I wouldn't be going back as I had failed my first year. That was fun. I needed some stability. A sturdy waypoint where I could emotionally recharge and rebuild. That was Ruby. She had her own place so I hadn't had to spend too much time at my parents' house. Being back at my parents' house was excruciatingly painful. Every time I walked along that top corridor, I was acutely reminded that my graduation photo would never be featured alongside the rest of the great family photographs as I had once fantasised. It was a daily visual reminder of my absolute failure.

I never envisaged a long-term future with Ruby. I was quickly driven to irritation by her discussions about 'Coronation Street' whilst she was on the phone to one of her sisters. I had gone from discussing the pertinent points of Taoist philosophy to being sat on a small sofa watching irrelevant crap on the television with a running commentary. Still, it was better than suffering the disappointed faces of Mother and Father every day. Ruby and I split up once. About a year after I had left university, I decided to join the Army. Ruby had no interest in following me around the country to wherever I'd be sent. We split on good terms, but after a brief attempt at a military career, I quickly found myself back in her bed. I'd never really left it since then.

Two months after I had parted company with service life, Ruby slapped a positive pregnancy test down on my morning newspaper. She was overjoyed; I was devastated. I was twenty-two years old, a failed student, a failed soldier and now I was going to be a father. The shock made me feel sick. Not only because of the imminent responsibility but because of the serious long-term attachment to Ruby that it would bring. Upon telling my father about the situation he just sighed, then walked to the drinks cabinet and poured a large single malt for himself. He didn't offer one to me.

His words of wisdom were,

"You've made your bed now lad, so now you are going to have to lie in it." I didn't expect comforting words from my father, and I didn't get any. "About time you got your head out of the clouds and started living in the real world. Get a job, knuckle down and get a proper place to live. You need to buck your ideas up and stop dreaming." All of his words were very, very helpful …

So, I got a job, a normal job in a plain old office building. I became a father, to a boy we called Isaac. Ruby and I rented a house together, and I sat in it and watched crap television whilst I listened to one-sided conversations.

Nine years passed. I had kept up my duties. I had kept a roof over our heads, kept food on the table, ensured all the bills were paid. Being able to pay the bills became more of a challenge when child number two arrived on the scene, but I managed it due to my stable and completely uninteresting job. Things between me and Ruby were in a perpetual state of decline even as child number three joined the clan. I had hoped that marrying her would have improved things, but it hadn't. She was a devoted and loving mother, but she just annoyed the fuck out of me, all the time. She'd continually devise new diet and exercise plans but only stuck to them for a day or two. When she would quit on some new ill-conceived project, she would blame me and my unsupportive attitude for her lack of success. But then in a few days time she would read a new article online and commence another new programme. I tried to keep her happy but it was such an exhausting and expensive effort because she didn't know what she was ever trying to achieve herself. She always needed a new gadget: a treadmill, an exercise bike, motivational books or diet pills. Her demands were formulated anew every couple of weeks, and she wouldn't cease her petition until she got what she wanted, however ridiculous.

Life was a maelstrom of catastrophe hidden behind a façade of fatherhood and husbandry. Whatever I did was wrong, doing nothing was normally worse. At least I still had cigarettes!

I had spent many weekends at work, even though I had no work to do. I would just go into the office, log on, and spend my day reading random Reddit articles or descending down YouTube tunnels. Spending Saturdays and Sundays in this way was far more preferable than spending the time at home with her. My perspective on the week was inverted; I looked forward to Monday mornings and dreaded the weekends. Christmas was the worst time of all. I couldn't wait to get back into the office in January.

I had a little ritual every day after my commute home. Before I would walk in through the front door, I would take a few seconds and close my eyes, and I'd remember B. I'd see the light fall over her face and recall the scent of her hair. The daily recollection had helped to keep me alive over the years. I had kept the same mobile number I had had back at university just in case B ever wanted to get in touch; then I would be ready. It was possible, and the possibility was all I needed. As long as she was alive the possibility existed that she would get in touch, that we could somehow be together again. I clung to that possibility with every breath. Without that I didn't know what I'd do. Well, without that and the pub.

{Chapter 24}

|A Day at the Office|

I drove to work that morning the same way I'd driven a thousand times before. After the standard battle for a parking space, I got out and locked the car, the standard orange flicker and twin beeps let me know that it was secure. I strolled to my office building and boarded the elevator. I rolled the office key fob around my hand as I ascended in the lift to my place of work. I wondered about the history of the fob. *"How many other hands had it been in? How many hands would it be in after mine?"* After a moment's thought I resolved myself with the truth that I didn't care. I saw the red digital readout display the floor number, for a second I remembered looking at the time on my old clock the morning I had left for university. I exhaled a silent sigh of sadness. Back in reality I saw my destination floor tick round. I knew I must walk off and conduct my daily activities. I did the only thing I could: I walked off, and entered the grave of daily life.

Lunch was a bland tuna salad with mayonnaise that I'd consume at my desk. I'd lazily feed myself with it as I stared off into space. Often whilst lost amongst the memories and mistakes of my youth I would hear Cherry say, "Cheer up Pete, there's plenty of people out there in the world who've got it a lot worse than you." I would give her a sigh complemented with an accompanying vacuous stare. I felt my reply matched her character, if you could call it character. Cherry was the latest graduate to join the 'team'. She was a lean bitch-faced twenty-one-year-old, but she possessed the wisdom of a much younger woman. I would muse to myself about her deluded and righteous state of mind, incredulous that she felt capable of passing judgement over me. There were no doubt people out there objectively worse off than me. *"Why should that be a source of optimism for me?"* I hadn't had the stimulus of narcotics for many years so I tried to analyse the issue with the mindset of a failed junior Philosophy student.

First, people other than me who felt bad either as a group or individually could only lead to a more negatively-charged world. A more negative world is not something I should logically take a positive outlook on or from.

Second, being told that lots of people in the world are not as well off as I am just plainly didn't cheer me up. So I have either failed to understand some deep point about the statement, or I did understand it but it didn't have the desired effect. Either route equalled a failure and a negative output.

Third, given the outcome of the previous two deductions I should feel guilty about not being able to put my situation into perspective. I don't feel guilty, so that makes me a societal 'bad' person.

None of my deductions led me to a point whereby being told that other people in the world had it worse than me was a good thing. I enjoyed being lost in the realms of rational thought for a while during the day. Apart from my daily remembering of B, it helped to keep me going.

"Peter," came the shrill voice of Mr. Hague.

"Yes Sir," I snapped back in an autonomic state.

"Have you finished the paperwork on the Williams account?"

"It will be done by this afternoon," I called across the office.

"Okay, I need it finalised by four o'clock," came the voice of pompously styled mediocre middle-management.

"No worries," I yelled back. Despite having not started any of it at the time.

I always tried to keep my conversations with him as brief as possible. He would often try to start up some sort of military themed conversation with me. He was the Officer Commanding of some local Army Cadet unit and he fucking loved it. Naturally I had played upon my time in the military during my interview because I really needed a job. When I saw his face light up at the talk of uniformed service, I knew it was a good sign. He spent about half of the interview telling me about all the camps he had been on. I had looked enthralled whilst I listened to his turbo-poon dits. He had a real hard-on at the prospect of having someone work for him who understood Army acronyms and abbreviations. I was ludicrously underqualified for the position I had interviewed for, what with not having a university degree and all. Any leg-up I could get would be worthwhile. At the end of the interview Mr. Hague offered me the job, with the caveat that I would become an adult instructor at his unit. That was over ten years ago and since then I had managed to avoid any formal interaction with his cadet lot. Fortunately, he hadn't pressed me on any uniformed issue that day. After giving me the deadline for the Williams account, he had called Cherry into his office, no doubt to talk about something regarding equality and diversity.

At 15:30 I handed in all of the Williams account papers to Mr. Hague. I went to the lift with fob in hand. I was headed for the roof. Smoking on the roof was by far the best part of my working day - usually it was the absolute best part of the entire day. A ten-minute lull when it was just me, a cold bench and the wind. I'd often put in my headphones and exhale to the notes of happier, naïve times. I'd travel back to a time when anything was possible. As I inhaled alone on the rooftop with the music of my youth forcing its way into my mind, I could almost recall how it felt to be young, to be happy, to be excited by the possibility of surprise. In my younger years I had thought that aging and becoming jaded was something that only happened to other people. It only happened to the kinds of men I had seen sitting silently across from me at one of the Llantarn pubs. Perhaps all those bequiffed of a romantic soul are destined to become such people. Perhaps they are all destined to end up as ornaments that never alter, save for the light of the alternating seasons. As I crushed the remnants of my cigarette around in the astray joined to the side of the bench, I felt the crushing of something inside myself. I headed back down to the office and had only one wish: *"Please just let me see out the rest of this day in peace."*

I walked back over to my desk and saw Cherry waiting there clutching some papers. The title paper bore large initials printed in a rainbow pattern that read, 'E and D'.

"Pete?" she asked with infuriating optimism before I could even be seated.

"Yes," I replied with the most neutral tone I could muster.

"As you are by far one of the oldest members of the junior staff here, I was hoping I could put you down to be one of the new equal opportunities and diversity monitors." She took my vexed and still expression as an invitation to describe the role in greater detail. I genuinely didn't give a shit about anything she was saying. All I really caught in passing were words like 'initiative', and 'spearheading', and phrases like 'Priority with a capital P' and 'synergistic fusion'. When she finally shut up and asked me what I thought, I just simply and politely said, "No." I thought that was a reasonably succinct answer to the proposition; Cherry just thought I needed a little convincing.

"I think that taking on this duty would look really good on your annual appraisal report."

Completely unable to restrain myself from retorting with all of the fake sincerity I could muster, I said in a higher pitch than normal,

"Really, do you really think so?" A small part of the forgotten joy that remained inside me lifted as I saw that she had mistaken my simulated enthusiasm for the genuine article.

"Yes I really do," she exclaimed as she lifted her pen from her clipboard in heightened expectation. I spoke to end the bullshit.

"Oh well in that case ... NO."

Cherry dejectedly turned her back to me and walked away. As she did, I thought two things. One, who needs INGSOC when you've got equal opportunities and diversity monitors. Two, I'd really love to fuck Cherry.

My final smoke of the working day took me on a little ten-minute stroll around town. I had my headphones in again as I always did for the walk. Ruined stone arches of deep historical significance, a few local shops, the bridge out to the back of town and finally back to the car park. I would always attempt to unwind just a little before I faced the true horror of the day: going home.

{Chapter 25}

|Perfect Nightmares and Dreams|

There are no words to describe the tedium of being trapped in a relationship that you hate.

At night, I would read books on quantum physics which theorised on the nature of reality. I would be forced to read them over the tune of the 'EastEnders' theme music. I was quite fond of the notion that all reality was a simulation: that way nothing really mattered, nothing was of consequence. In the same way that nothing you could do in a computer game actually mattered. I liked the notion, but couldn't bring myself to actually believe it. I just couldn't conceive of a mechanism that would be capable of synthetically creating the longing that I still had for B. I would carry on pondering such things long after her soaps had finished and she was left snoring on the sofa. I never hated Ruby, but I did pity her. She didn't have a creative, expansive or romantic mind. I could never discuss any meaningful topics with her. At least when the books and ideas faded and sleep took me, I had dreams.

Following our temporary reunification in Llantarn, B had not been in touch. I had messaged a few times and got no reply. I resolved myself to leave it there for the time being. She would communicate when she was ready. I had waited for emotional eons to hear from her the first time, if necessary I'd wait even longer to hear from her again. As a result, my dreams were the only place I could be with her, when I was lucky enough for my subconscious to bring us together. For years my dreams had been the only way for me to see her, all the way up till I actually got to see her again in the flesh, for those fleetingly brief days. I was used to having her only in my sleeping fantasy. They were the most vivid dreams anyone could ever know. Her skin, her smell, her tonal inflections were all perfect though I could never remember precisely what we had talked about. But content didn't matter. Perfection doesn't need a content or a context. If something is perfect, it is simply perfect beyond any form of parameter that can be measured. As such, her lips were so perfectly, damnably real. Our mystical kisses as real as any I had ever known. Just being with her in that realm was almost enough to ease all the pain of the years, all the self-admonishments and regrets. Sometimes during my dreams with her I would realise that I was dreaming, but rather than turn away from my imagined soulmate I would just tell myself that I wasn't dreaming, just to make the unsustainable play last another scene. If I were to ever fail in reassuring my sleeping self that the mirage before me was real, then the dream would be a pathetic nightmare. One in which I knew I was just a fool waiting for the dawn. Fortunately, I never fell into such a wretched state. My will to be with her at any cost, in any way, always triumphed over all possible realities.

One night back in Llantarn, amongst the hot air and hanging smoke of B's room, I had experienced a truly unique sleep experience. B and I had spent several hours doing what young couples in love do. We were sharing each other's saturated embrace awaiting the inevitability of sleep. With B in my arms I dropped into a void, a total void. It was an absence of space, time, consciousness, everything. I was reasonably well read on different religious experiences at the time, but this was nothing like anything I had read. The closest thing I could describe it as was a black nirvana. Yet the feeling was not one of illumination or enlightenment - far from it. It was the absence of all feeling, all perception. It was the nonexistence of absolutely everything, well, except one thing: peace. Peace in all of its possible connotations. A resolute tranquillity impossible to express in text. Rest, quiet, satisfaction, contentment; no synonym could ever relay the actual manifestation of the event. The incomprehension of being in a state devoid of dimension could only be summarised in one word: perfection. Perhaps the stars had aligned or the universe had decided to play a trick on me, but whatever it was it didn't last forever. When I awoke from that form, I had B curled up beautifully in my arms. She looked at me, kissed me and softly whispered, "I know."

I had experienced the feeling once again during the sleep I'd had after our beautiful reconnection that night in 'The White Lion'. The endless peace repeated. I knew I was immeasurably lucky. Most people would live their entire lives without any real spiritual epiphany to call their own. I had had it twice. Endless peace.

There are no words to describe the requiem of being trapped outside a relationship that you love.

{Chapter 26}

|Light Relief|

Sometimes in order to avoid the pressing pain of going home I'd get the opportunity to go to the pub. 'The Anchor and Axe' was not a particularly pleasant place. It was over-aged and felt generally sour. When the bloody smoking ban had been forced upon society it had essentially killed off the public house as I'd always known it. Gone were the times when a man could put a couple of quid in the juke box, sit with his pint and smoke his thoughts away. That was a beautiful activity that any free man should not be prevented from doing. A man sat alone, drinking, smoking, listening to his music reverberate around the walls of his favourite drinking establishment - truly a wonderful thing lost.

The nicotine yellow walls of 'The Anchor' still bore the memorial scars of such times. They also reminded me of my room in Hawson. 'The Anchor' was a tiny part of the country still holding onto older days, better days. Its enduringly passionate and hopeless connection with the past gave me hope. I liked it in there. Also, the fact that the landlord, 'Big Phill the Geordie', was a consummate chain smoker helped because after eleven o'clock in the evening he would lock the doors and bring out the ashtrays. When that happened, I was able to close my eyes and for entire minutes of my life, I could actually feel like I had gone back. I felt as though when I opened my eyes, I would realise that the last years were nought but a booze-fuelled hallucination. That I would open my eyes and see B, smoking right next to me. I was always disappointed by reality when it contrasted with my imaginings.

The lust for elder days extended out from the building itself into the psyches of the regular customers. They certainly had no love of the present day. They had also gifted me the nickname of 'The Boffin', due to my having to wear a suit to work in place of the usual factory overalls that adorned most of the pub's clientele. Once they had found out I had been to university as well then the name was cemented. I didn't oppose the title. I'd rather be known as 'The Boffin' than some of the other names that the more colourful individuals who frequented the establishment were referred to as. I felt relaxed in that place, borderline positive on the odd occasion, but nothing that ever approached actual happiness. Just enough confidence though to make me feel human after a few pints.

On common occasion, John would be in. John was a clever man, slightly younger and far more optimistic and organised than me. He had also had a short spell in the military but tired of it rapidly, finding life in the armed services incompatible with his tendency to use his initiative. I never completely got to the bottom of the exact circumstances of his departure from service life, but that was his business. He did however say that he had come into a particularly large inheritance at the time which may have played a part in his exit. I did know that he definitely had served though. He was not some Walter Mitty dreamer. At our first meeting I had probed him with some rather detailed and suitably varied questions about military life, training and doctrine. If he had been lying I would've known. Besides, he hadn't claimed to be some sort of super army soldier who had been on a dozen missions behind enemy lines like most of them did. He had been in the Royal Engineers. All of his answers to my enquires were expansive and complete.

I had also asked him why he drank in 'The Anchor'; it wasn't the nicest of places and a good-looking young man such as him should probably be in one of the nicer, more trendy places in town. He simply said that he liked it in there because it kept him, "Grounded." Whatever he meant by that I didn't know, so I just accepted it. He was not native to the local area. He had moved north across the border almost as soon as he had been discharged. His logic was pretty sound: he would simply get more for his money around here. Which he had. He lived alone in a large house about a mile out of town, and spent his days reading, writing and studying his true love of history. We were kindred spirits to a point. He appreciated the fact that there was somebody well-versed in general knowledge that he could speak at length with, as did I. We spoke about all topics, all issues. When we were both in the bar, we would always sit together for the duration of the evening. At times his upbeat personality would get the better of me during an evening's drinking and I could feel his positivity cross over to me, right up until the point I'd wake up at home with a hangover.

One such evening, after another painstakingly numb day in the office, I walked into the pub, pushed through the loose swing door at the main entrance past the big front door, and entered the main lounge. As I approached the bar one of the regulars spoke loudly to announce my arrival,

"Ooooop, here comes 'The Boffin.'"

I smiled at the room with what I considered to be appreciative grace and made my way to the bar. To my delight John was already sat down at it. He had a pint in front of him which appeared to have only had a sip or two taken from it. Before I had the chance to greet him properly and pull up one of the stools to his side he had spoken over the bar to the barmaid on duty,

"Pint for 'The Boffin' please love." She cordially performed her duty in silence.

"Thanks very much mate," I said with genuine gratitude. The first time I had said something genuine and respectful to another person for quite some time. The dripping glass was placed down on the mat in front of me and I held it aloft. "Good health," I proclaimed.

"Good health," came John's echoed reply.

It was to be the first of many that night. That evening, he told me all about his new business venture. He was going to start his own military history tours company. He wouldn't be limited to the typical battlefield tours of Normandy or Belgium; he was going to do more historic tours in the UK too. I wasn't convinced that people would queue up to tour English Civil War battlefields or medieval scraps over forts that now existed as rubble between farmers' fields, but it wasn't my money getting thrown at it. I didn't pay it too much attention. After a few more drinks I wanted to talk to him about something else.

"So, John, you probably don't remember me talking about B."

"You must be joking mate!" he cut me off. "Every time you have more than four you bring her up," he scoffed with a warm chuckle. He went on, "I don't know what you're so hung up about. It was years and years ago now. You were just kids really in the larger scheme of life. You're married now with three kids. You have a steady and stable job. You provide for your family. Have you any idea just how lucky you are? To most men in the world you have a fairy-tale life. Yet you still cling onto the past with every emotional sinew that you possess. Just imagine the life you'd have if you put all that energy into the family you do have instead of a dream that's never going to happen." He stopped for breath and finished his current pint, then ordered us two more. His point was compelling, even striking. I replied with the only bit of personal philosophy I had taken away from Llantarn. It was a drunken and fuzzy dictation of my thesis.

"Well, John. You make a valid point. But all of those people you describe as being jealous of my life are not me. They are external to the system that is my life. I am the only one living my life; I am the only person I have to justify anything to. So, how I feel, or what I deduce about any scenario in my life is purely an effort of my own being. There is no jury to debate my actions, intentions or feelings, just a judge, one judge: me. The only thing that counts to that judge is the possibility of being happy. As long as I am alive, and B is alive, there is a statistical possibility of us being together, that equates to a statistical possibility of me being happy. Since no one else can know what I feel or think then their opinions on it may well be valid, be informed, be well-reasoned, but ultimately irrelevant." I stopped for breath and took a gulp out of the fresh pint before me.

John replied, "Well, when you put it like that…" He followed that up with a shrug, though he continued his quizzical thought process. "But I just don't get how you can have such strong feelings for someone you haven't seen since university - that was like what, nearly twenty years ago." He looked perplexed.

"Err, yeah, not quite that long as it happens," I revealed to him sheepishly.

Eleven o'clock arrived and 'Big Phill the Geordie' bounded down the stairs to relieve the barmaid. As soon as she was gone the door was locked, the ashtrays were out, and better times resumed. John and I demoted ourselves from the bar to a comfy table and talked more.

"What do you mean you went back to Wales and saw her?" John asked.

"Well, quite simply, I went back to Wales and saw her," I said drolly. John looked at me, obviously unimpressed by my explanation. Without him saying anything more I expanded properly. "So, I never changed my mobile number since being a student. I always thought that maybe if I kept it the same that she would still be able to get in touch with me if she wanted to. One day, she did."

"So, she just messaged you right out of the blue then?" he asked.

"Well, yeah. We messaged a bit, I told her about Ruby and the kids, she told me about her new fella, 'Roy', and then she proposed meeting up."

John turned from his seat and shouted to the Geordie landlord.

"Can we get two triple whiskeys over here please boss?"

'Big Phill', being a man of few words, merely replied in his deep Novocastrian voice, "Aye, reet."

We sat quaffing whiskey and smoking, tapping our ash into an old Vaux ashtray. I told him all of the particulars of seeing her again. He seemed amazed that I hadn't brought it up before now. It had been almost a year ago at that point. I just said, "I hadn't really felt like telling anyone else. I just wanted to keep those few days to myself for as long as I could."

John asked, "So, why tell me now?" I didn't have a good answer. But I did have an honest one.

"I just felt like it. I guess I needed to talk to someone about it, I needed someone else to know about it. Not that it will ever change anything. I just felt that it was a pressure valve that I needed to release."

John was very understanding, he simply replied with, "Okay." John then put his cards on the table. "You know Pete, I don't much like women."

I looked at him oddly.

"No, no, I don't mean that I am that way inclined. I just mean that I can't be doing with all the drama, all the administration that's involved with that kind of thing. I am more than happy being on my own. It's just so much simpler, so much easier. I like having my quiet life." He seemed content with himself as he sipped away at the golden fluid in his glass.

"Have you ever been in love?" I asked him.

"Um, no, I don't think so," he replied in an uncaring fashion.

"It's worth all the heartache and misery, all the struggle and turmoil. You might be sat there feeling smug with yourself that you aren't me, but I am sat here just pitying you."

John certainly did not appreciate that comment. The atmosphere between us took a rapid and dark turn.

"I think you've had enough to drink for one night Pete."

"Oh fuck off ya prick, you're not my father!" I spat out with venom.

"No, he left for the Riviera with your mum after they'd seen how much of a fuck-up you've become."

I punched him squarely in the face, mainly because I was drunk and he was right. His nose exploded and I instantly felt bad. I knew I had just been a total dick. My pissed-up volatile monkey-child had lashed out, and I couldn't take it back.

'Big Phill' gave instructions to us in his undebatable voice.

"How, get out ma fuckin pub right now the pair o ye. And divint come back!"

I stood up and left without looking back. I never saw or spoke to John again, nor would I ever see again the inside of 'The Anchor and Axe'.

I stumbled into my dark house at about three in the morning. I managed to make my way upstairs probably making lots of noise. I decided it would be best to sleep in the spare room, as I was no doubt going to be in the firing line from Ruby in the morning. Best not wake her just yet. I undressed and carelessly dropped all of my clothes wherever they fell. I got into bed. I was very, very drunk.

As I set the alarm on my phone, I noticed that alongside the multitude of missed calls and messages from the wife I also had a text from an unknown number. It was too blurry to read with my intoxicated eyes. It would have to wait till morning. I passed out.

{Chapter 27}
|The Last Full Day and Night|

After I read that message the next morning, and found out that she was gone, I knew there was only one thing I could do. It was good of Roy to let me know what had happened. Without him having told me, I don't know how, or when I would have found out. Perhaps, eventually, I would have taken her persistent lack of contact as a slight and just turned up at her door only to find out about her death then. Either way, my unspeakable anguish was only alleviated by my certainty of action.

That morning, Ruby decided to give me the silent treatment - an ideal scenario in truth. I sorted myself out in the spare room and left for work as normal, though with a handful of paracetamol, ibuprofen and aspirin to try and bat down my outrageous hangover. I had lots to do; I needed as clear a head as possible. Though I had departed for work I never turned up: I had far more important tasks to perform. I went to the bank.

After ensuring that all of the funds at my discretion were transferred into the joint account and double checking the small print in my life insurance policy I went to go and see my solicitor.

I was lucky to get in without an appointment, but in I got. All my affairs were then put in final order. Following that, I went home. The kids were at school and Ruby was working her part-time job as a teaching assistant at the local adult education centre. I had the house to myself. I took off my suit, put on my favourite shorts and my most comfortable hoodie.

I sat down at the kitchen table with a fresh paper notepad and a crisply sharp pencil. I had letters to write; and if these were to be the last written words I'd ever produce then they would be physically etched in the way that best reflected my experience of writing. As I felt the graphite cut into the paper I could have almost been a student sat in a lecture again. The beauty of that impure symmetry was quickly lost in the content of what it was that I actually had to write.

I wrote a letter to my parents. I attempted to explain my actions as best I could. They would never understand my justifications but at least after they had read it I wouldn't be able to disappoint them anymore. Following that goodbye message, I wrote four more letters, one for each of the children and one for Ruby. With the letters complete I walked along to the nearest post box and sent the one to my parents on its way. Ruby would hopefully keep faithful custody of the kids' letters till they were old enough to at least try and understand. On the walk back I stopped in at the local shop and bought the best red wine that I could, and four packs of my favourite cigarettes.

The rest of the day was my own. I slumped myself down on the sofa. I had a super-secret emergency stock of weed that I'd been harbouring for years. I brought it out to enjoy alongside the wine. I watched a medley of various film and TV scenes on YouTube. Scenes that had emotional significance and meaning to me. I listened to songs from my favourite albums; I read passages from my favourite books. I smoked, I drank, I smoked, I cried, I was happy, I was sad, I was a mess - it was the most alive I'd felt since last seeing B.

Around five in the afternoon, Ruby and the kids came home. They found a degenerate mess of a father and husband in the family lounge. Ruby told the kids to just get back in the car because they were going to stay with Granny and Grampa that night. Once they were resecured in the car Ruby came back through to speak to me. Well, it was more of a shout.

"What the fuck is wrong with you!" she aimed right at me. I didn't answer; I didn't see the point. "All I have ever done is love you. All your kids have ever done is love you. Why are you always so distant, so absent?" She was welling up and emotionally aggressive.

All I could think to say was, "Because I am." The truth wasn't something she'd have wanted to hear, nor would it have made things any easier for either of us at that point.

"Why can you never just fucking talk to me? Why do you find it easier to stay out all night drinking and talking to half-strangers in pubs than you do to talk to your own wife?"

I didn't want the conversation to go any longer. I did the only thing I knew how to do with her: I lied.

"Listen, you take the kids over to your folks' place and stay there with them tonight. Tomorrow night we will have an evening together, just you and me, and I will tell you absolutely everything. But can you just give me until then to get all of my thoughts in check, please." I pleaded with all the sincerity I could manage. Fortunately, it worked. She just shook her head, shouted, "Fine!" and left the house. She slammed the front door as she went. Her car engine rattled into life and they were gone.

Now was my chance; my opportunity to get as seriously fucked-up as possible, to bring back that old Llantarn spirit! I crushed up some old Tramadol I had stowed away from years ago after I'd broken my arm, mixed it with a bit of Co-codamol, and the pollen residue I had left over from grinding down the weed. I lined up six or seven generous lines and helped myself. I also ingested a tab, a special tab that I had kept hidden since my Llantarn days. It was from the night when Kof had gone missing. He'd taken too much and disappeared leaving nothing behind him but an irregular dispersal of luminous blue paint… but that's another story. *"No point not dropping it now,"* I thought. It instantly dissolved on my tongue whilst the fair notes of Pink Floyd, Dire Straits played on. One bottle of wine was gone, another was opened. I started to feel mentally unusual, like I was drifting off into a sub-conscious realm. I liked it. I tried to consciously encourage my mind to let go and get lost in it, and away it went.

It was a waking dream, a waking lucid dream of some sort of party. A party in which I was the star attraction. All those in attendance seemed to be there because of some sort of connection to me. In fact, I couldn't see anyone there that I didn't know. Before I knew it I was centre-stage in front of them all. The pupils and teachers from Woodbourne clapped with Henrietta as Mr. Demptham lead them all on. The entire student population of Llantarn applauded and cheered. All of the lads from the regiment were there in best dress uniform, they whistled and jeered. Everyone from the office hooted and howled for me. The regulars from 'The Anchor and Axe' were all there with jars raised. My mother, my father, they smiled at me. Every last one of them, dressed in their finest regalia. All of them existed in their ideal state. Each of them grinned widely, laughed loudly, oozed positivity and love. All of it aimed toward me, Peter Morgan, at the magical crest of his life. An attraction in his own ego, it was marvellous. It was an abstract assembly of pure flattered joy. Beautiful lights and all the alternative pomp on parade for the most epic epitaph that any man could have wished for.

I had always yearned to live a life worthy of romantic obituary; well, that nonsensical theatrical festival was my life's romance brought to impossible life. I was front and centre of my own existence.

There was no B. I understood that this was a farewell from the living, wishing me well on my journey to the other side. This was the final curtain, the concluding cut, and the only thing I could do was take a bow to the rapture, in the soaring, uplifting noise.

150

{Chapter 28}

|Peter Morgan, Thesis for Life|

Start of Thesis:

1. Only I can know when I am truly and honestly happy, because nobody else is me.

2. As long as the statistical possibility of being truly, honestly happy exists, I must live.

3. Nothing/nobody can rationalise or justify the requirement to continue life to me without the possibility of true and honest happiness.

4. I can only be truly and honestly happy with B.

5. As long as there is a statistical possibility of me being with B, then there is a statistical possibility of me being truly, honestly happy.

6. If there is no statistical possibility of being truly, honestly happy then there is no fundamentally compelling reason to live, because;

7.   i. Life is knowable, measurable, understandable. Post-death existence is not.

     ii. If statistical possibility of true, honest happiness in life drops to zero, then the only place that true, honest happiness can exist is after life.

     iii. True, honest happiness either exists in some form of after-life or not.

     iv. True, honest happiness is a 0.5 possibility after death. It either exists, or it doesn't.

     v. 0.5 is infinitely larger than 0.

     vi. In this case, true, honest happiness is infinitely more possible in a state of death than in a state of life.

8. So long as B is alive, I must stay alive.

9. If B dies before I do, I must die to increase my possibility for true, honest happiness.

10. The only person I have to justify this thesis to is myself, because everyone else isn't me.

End of Thesis:

{Chapter 29}
|Mourning Has Broken|

I woke to an empty house: no wife, no children, no party of well-wishers. I did have some company though; another splitting headache. I thought it apt enough as it matched my heartache. I pulled myself upright on the sofa, upon which I had slept. Stale smoke filled the room and spots of ash dotted the carpet. An empty wine glass stood proudly on the table with several empty bottles strewn over the floor. Echoes of my subconscious carnival still painted images in my mind, still played sounds in my ears. "Some party," I jested to myself.

I looked over at the clock to see the time. It didn't really matter, but it did again remind me of how fastidiously I had checked the time on my old digital clock in my room on the morning that I'd left for Llantarn. This time I revelled in the temporal symmetry. That time-check was right before a big adventure too. I felt virtually no connection between that young man who was so full of ambition, yearning, excitement and hope. Well, I still had hope at least. I wanted to laugh at the mental image of my younger self on that morning, but I couldn't. I was too jealous of him, and to deface his memory in such a way, it would have been exceedingly bad form! I did the only thing I could possibly do in that moment, I lit up a cigarette. I coughed gratuitously after the first puff, but persisted till I could inhale properly.

I had a simple and easy plan for the day, nothing complicated about it. I had foreseen this possible course of events many times over the years, especially in my darker hours. I knew what had to happen. Still, I felt slightly nervous; it was a big gamble, though the gamble was logical. I had had such thoughts before, and I was always calmed by the two possible end-states. Either there was nothing after death, and I wouldn't feel anything, so that state didn't matter, or she would be there waiting for me. Either way was acceptable, not just acceptable, but preferable.

I rose off the sofa and went upstairs to get dressed - I still wanted to be smart whatever happened. I put on my best suit, my finest shirt. I had kept my old Army issue shoes since my discharge and had worn them most days to the office. To the untrained eye they just looked like a normal pair of Oxfords, they were good enough for me. As I tied the laces up tightly for the final time, they gave me an element of confidence about what was to come, almost a stiff upper lip with regards to my mental approach to the day, this day of all days. I checked myself in the mirror, I was smart. I walked downstairs, went outside, closed the door behind me, locked it for the last time. I knew the insurance money would be sufficient to pay off the mortgage - funny to think that in order to own the home my family lived in I would have to die. It was paradoxical and comical in equal measure.

My walking pace was quite brisk considering the hangover and lack of food. I kept my strides long and swift all the way to the bridge. I couldn't remember the last time I had intentionally walked somewhere without having headphones in my ears blaring away. I had hoped it would be a pleasant, light and airy experience, one in which I heard the softness of the winds dancing round green branches, but it wasn't. It was just the periodic passing of diesel engines intermixed with the occasional person shouting and the gangly squawk of hungry seagulls.

My life had changed so much since I was a boy, and not for the better. It mattered not. I reached my destination, the bridge. I must have walked that way hundreds of times, driven it thousands, but today it looked different. It wasn't a bridge anymore; it was a gate. I leisurely strolled down to the halfway point. The only other souls I saw were a young mother pushing a buggy across the other side. Once she had passed me, I owned the bridge – well, for pedestrians at least. The endless onslaught of cars proceeded continuously.

There were no gasps or inhalations of despair as I clambered up onto the edge: there were no people there to make them, and I hoped it would stay that way. I knew I'd need to run through it all again in my head once I got up there. I might even draw a small crowd in the time it took me to do it. Maybe an audience was what I secretly wanted. If my extra-neurological hootenanny last night was anything to go by, perhaps I did want to go out with people noticing.

I climbed up. Up to the edge, up to the end.

{Chapter 30}
|Leap of a Lifetime|

So here it is at last. She is dead. The only thing that made me a better man is gone. My course of action is now clearer than ever. I developed my thesis based on *my* mind and how *I* felt, how *I* still feel. I will hold true, I will. Having crept back all the way from my school days till this very morning I feel that I have ticked every box. There are no words that can stop me. I just need to let Newton do his work.

With my arms raised I turn my head one last time to regard my audience. Amongst the police uniforms and anxious faces, I see myself.

The eighteen-year-old me, the one who treasured his secret smokes in the walled garden orchards at Woodbourne. The very same boy who read Wordsworth with such hope.

Next to him is the dazed nineteen-year-old who is full of shame and regret, with long uncombed hair and a multi-coloured hoodie. A face completely saturated with the deep scars of lost potential.

Next to him, the twenty-one-year-old. Wearing Her Majesty's proud green uniform with virtually no hair, all broad shoulders and steely eyes. Those metallic eyes melted only by the fire of extreme operational misfortune.

The next me is the office worker. Dull eyes and fully broken demeanour.

They all know the same as me: that this is right. They all smile at me. They know the logic, they know the reason, they are all smoking! The sight makes me smile to myself, thinking back to all the people who'd told me not to smoke because of cancer. Ha! If I only have to justify my actions to myself, then it looks like all of my selves approve.

I respond to all of my phantasms with a smile and a nod, only distantly aware of Ruby's voice screaming in desperation. The time is nigh. The leap of faith, the leap of hope is here.

With a smile on my face I lean forward as a dead weight. It reminds me of one of those falls that you do as a trust exercise on some bullshit corporate management training day. The distant yells and screams intensify as they all see me pass the point of no return. I pay them no heed. They are not me after all.

That cold flowing Scottish water is rushing toward me now, so fast, nearly as fast as falling in love. My life doesn't flash before my eyes, only her face. Her face from the first night I saw it, the first time I fell in love, the only time I fell in love. I close my eyes.

The drop continues, but as I fall, I smile. From start to end I smile.

I hit the water.

'Woodbourne'

'Old Hall Building'

'Hawson Hall'

'The Royal Ivy'

'B'

'The Circle'

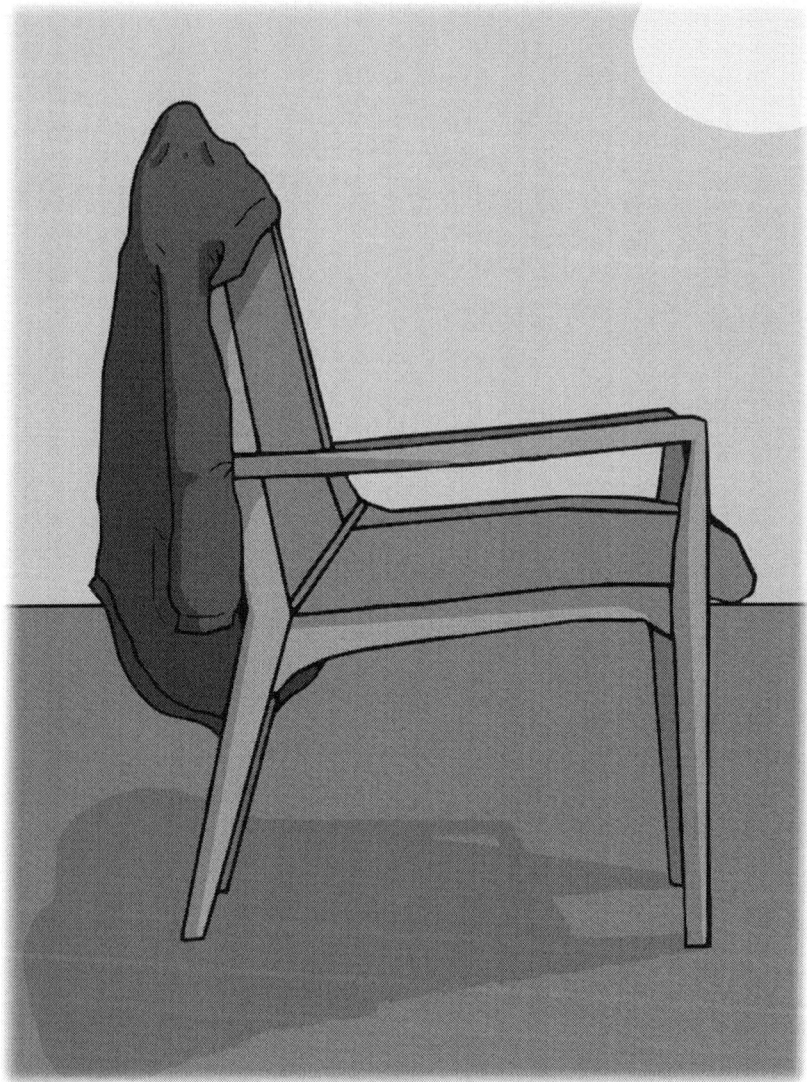

'*Jacket on the Chair*'

'Relative Bench'

'Hawson Cell Block'

'Smoking for Peace'

'The Final Barscape'

{Chapter 0 conc.}
|I Smile|

The warm sun beams down upon my face as I cross the footbridge joining one side of the campus to the other. I see her sitting there on a red tartan blanket; perfect poetry in stillness. She is set upon the deep, lush, vividly green grass. I stop walking and just stare at her as I lean over the rail. She looks up at me and sees me watching her. She gently places her book down and pats on the blanket next to her, beckoning me to sit.

For now, all I can do is stand on the bridge and smile at her, as she smiles at me.

'As she smiles at me'

Afterword

Primarily, I would just like to thank you for reaching the end of my story. If you are still reading now, then I suppose you won't mind reading some of my thoughts regarding it.

So, you may well think that there are quite a few loose ends such as how did B die? What happened to Peter in the Army? Well, I have absolutely no plan to answer any of these. This is because they don't really matter. I did have lots more material written up about such things but during the editing process I realised that they didn't matter. I felt like including them would have just been filler with no real point. Does it matter that I always imagined Peter's drinking friend John as being of Caribbean descent? I don't think so. The back story behind lots of characters has been cut out because I didn't think they added anything to the real story. And the real story is all about Peter's flawed reasoning. This is the real essence of the story. The fact that you only have to justify your actions to yourself, and you are the one in control of what those actions are. I do realise the obvious further justifications required by society, such as the requirement to follow the law. Yet as plainly stated, those requirements are not formed by the individual, but by the society in which the individual lives. In our current society suicide is the biggest killer of men under forty, and though I am not suicidal in any way, I thought that now more than ever it was important to explore certain feelings related to how men in this most modern era may feel.

As a society we are not really as advanced as we would like to think we are - in fact we are less than a hundred years away from a very real class and gender

orientated society. I think that some of the attitudes of that era still pervade (for better or worse) in the modern male psyche. Notions of duty and family responsibility still reside in the mind of many men in the contemporary world, and I feel that they cannot reconcile their feelings of duty with their own duty to themselves to actually live a life that makes them happy. In this regard I attempted to show Peter in this trapped state. Unable to leave his wife and children to be on his own and face the unknowns of the world. No doubt he would have left in a heartbeat for his true love B, but anything other than that was not a viable option due to the lifetime of uncertainty and societal scorn he felt that would oppress him. B was the only entity that existed that gave him the strength to look past such hurdles. In the end, he did the only thing he felt he could do, which he could justify to himself in perpetuity.

I'd like to make a few comments about the layout of the book. Originally, I had planned to have fewer chapters that lasted much longer. After reading a copy of 'The Martian' by Andy Weir', I saw how powerful and easy it was to read lots of smaller chapters. I feel the structure makes it much easier to read, especially for people who would not normally read a novel. So, if you were pondering why the structure is so rapid then now you know.

When it came to the illustrations at the end of the book, I had originally planned to have them all split up and distributed throughout the relevant chapters that they refer to, but it just didn't fit somehow. I decided to place them right at the end so it could effectively recap the events that brought Peter to hit the water. I feel it is poignant because as Peter is falling his life doesn't flash before his eyes, but after he hits the water, maybe it does.

The conclusion of chapter 0 I leave to the interpretation of the reader.

Finally, although this text may deal with some very serious topics, it is not meant to be taken as a justification for anyone to take their own life. It is a hypothetical work of fiction and by no means meant to be used as a guidebook to killing oneself. If you, dear reader, do feel as though you may cause harm to yourself or others then please pick up the phone and seek help. There is no shame in admitting that a struggle is taking place. If an army is losing a battle it doesn't just fight and die, it sends out for allies and wins the war. Win your war.

Acknowledgements

Well, wow! I finally managed to cobble together this story and get it into print. Thanks very much for fingering your way through it and getting to this point. I hope I have been able to engage at least one emotional or logical thought in you by reading through it. If I have then the book has served its purpose. But this book has been approximately seven years in the making and as such there are seven years of acknowledgements to make, so go ahead and strap yourself in.

As I am sure that about 90-95% of the people reading this are purely reading it because they know me and are curious, I will try and name as many of those people as possible. (Loz, I know you are reading it just so you can find fault with it!) If you don't see your name in print here then, sorry, you just don't matter to me very much, get over it. So, to begin at the beginning.

I couldn't have written this without the people who make pencils in factories. I wrote every word of this up first on paper with a pencil so my thanks go to all who work in the factories making them. I would also like to sincerely thank Rothmans tobacco company for keeping me well stocked up with their finest quality cigarettes for the duration of the write/type up. I couldn't possibly mention the fags without the booze, so for that my thanks go to Barefoot wine for keeping me nicely topped up with Merlot throughout. If truth be known, I was drunk pretty much the whole time I knocked this up…in truth…I am drunk now…anyway…

Onto the more practical thanks now. Jade and our girls, thanks so much for all the understanding you've shown this project down the line, you know I love you xxx.

Now, lots of my acquaintances are very shy so I will thank them using first names only. Mum and Dad thanks a heap, this laptop came in real handy for playing games and for writing up novels that hardly anyone will ever read, thanks a bunch again. When it comes to having a good boss, the big baldy jocktastic Al is hard to beat! So, thanks for all the leeway you've given me over the years. In fact, thanks to everyone in the big 'five-four' for just making work a tolerable place to be for eight hours a day. Special thanks go to the special team, ya'll know it's the place to be. All hail the pattern spotters and puzzle masters.

Right, people who actually helped with the book. Well, I have to thank the glorious Lydia for doing a lot of the initial editing work for me. Lydia, you have always been, and continue to be what I perceive as the personification of art. Please never stop doing what you do, I love you so much as I am sure all those do who know you and/or have the pleasure to work with you. Next up we have Julia, who at the time I am writing this up is currently awaiting her new baby, hope it won't be too long now. Thanks for giving your input in the proofreading stage. I also have to mention Sam B, long time college with similar literary ambitions. Sam, thanks for not mocking my ideas and occasionally looking at stuff for me. (Sam, I still hate you for throwing me under the bus that time).

Next up, we have the DABC. Thanks for making me feel part of something real. A particularly solemn mention has to go to Paul Kavanagh, who unfortunately passed away before the publishing of this book. He was a natural talent in the ring and possessed a heart of solid gold. As such this novel is dedicated to you, so save me a seat at whatever bar you're at and have one waiting for me when I get there! To Jack, thanks for always being up for a monumental session, they always help with the creative juices. Your sheer inability to say 'no' to alcohol has been a mighty support to me in ways that you will never know. In that vein, many thanks to all the S'n'S group, thanks for continually serving up booze and always always always abiding by the responsible social distancing of our time… There are too many characters to list from that hallowed hall, but suffice to say, I miss some of you, and look forward to better times when we can all sit around together again. Oh, I cannot forget Fi, thanks for all the toasties.

Mr Sebastian Gibson. The amazingly talented and unbelievably lazy illustrator for this work has been sort of helpful, from time to time, I suppose. Which is all I can really expect from someone who doesn't know he isn't getting paid any of the proceeds from this book...Just kidding Seb, your cheque is in the post...lol...Hope to see you soon for pipes, tweed and ale. This list must end with Joe. Joe W, thanks so much for everything that you didn't think was a big deal. You are a much better friend than I ever deserved. You are missed.

Anyone wishing to get in contact for any reason, please email me at;

lmhutton01@gmail.com

That's all folks. Just remember not to take life too seriously and have that extra glass of wine now and again. If you *can* laugh then laugh, if you can't laugh, laugh anyway.

L.M. Hutton

Printed in Great Britain
by Amazon